I0594423

Also by DJ Geribo

The House at the Top of the Trees

Eddie Easel and the Case of the Missing Green

The Miracle Dog

Mouse Bound

All titles available from BBD Publishing at www.bbdpublishing.com.

Selected titles available on Amazon in softbound and e-book formats.

SEVEN
STORIED
HOUSES

SEVEN STORIED HOUSES

DJ Geribo

BBD Publishing ~ Alton, NH

Copyright © 2018 by DJ Geribo

All rights reserved. Except as permitted under U.S. Copyright Act of 1976, no part of this publication may be reproduced, distributed, or transmitted in any form or by any means, or stored in a database or retrieval system, without the prior written permission of the publisher.

Seven Storied Houses is published by

BBD Publishing
P.O. Box 351
Alton, NH 03809

www.BBDPublishing.com

Book Layout and Editing by James J. Fontaine

Cover Design by Positively Creative Solutions, LLC

Illustrations Copyright by the Individual Artists as Credited

Printed in the United States of America

10 9 8 7 6 5 4 3 2 1

Library of Congress Control Number: 2018941120

ISBN 978-0-9883068-4-4

TABLE OF CONTENTS

Preface

I've always had this thing about houses. When I'm traveling by car and if I'm not reading, which is how I usually pass time as a passenger, I'll look at the houses we pass on the way to wherever it is we are going. I will imagine who lives there and the life they may lead. What do they look like? Are they young or old? Married or widowed? Do they have kids? Are they happy? Do they eat at McDonalds or enjoy home-cooking? Do they watch TV every night or read or play a family game? Or do they partake in something more sinister or more educational? The questions go on and on. I imagine that I'm mostly wrong in my conclusions. But sometimes I think I am spot on.

What is it about houses that can define who we are? Someone I know recently told me about the house they live in, "in the richest community in the world." I looked it up – she was right. But why did she have to send me a photo of her house and add the comment about the level of wealth needed to live in her community? Did this make her a more valuable person in society? What did her house say about her? What kinds of insecurities was she trying to hide behind? What was she trying to convince herself was true about the person she was?

We do judge people by the house they live in. We do think we know who they are and what they are like. They are rich or poor, slobs or neat-freaks, over-consumers or minimalists. We can tell all this by seeing their house and the neighborhood where they live. We think we know them. We think we know about the life they lead.

But all we really know is the house they live in. We don't know what goes on behind closed doors. We don't know how they may suffer, if they are happy, if they cry and are sad, or if they love like no one has ever loved before. We can only surmise. And we very well may be wrong.

Knowing all this, I still needed to pursue my fascination with the variety of houses that I pass by on my travels and write my own story about the lives that are lived inside. Some may be true, some not. But they are my stories and what I imagine goes on behind some closed doors.

To the Artists

A special thank you goes to each of the artists who contributed their artwork to represent the houses in these stories. At the back of this book you will find a brief bio for each artist along with their contact information. The artists are:

> Cori Caputo
> Barbara Carlson
> Mark Cowper
> Mary Frances Smith

Although a couple of the illustrations are my own, my strengths as an artist are in painting wildlife, nature, and animal portraits. For professional pen and ink house portraits or similar illustration work, I highly recommend contacting any of these fine artists.

Special Acknowledgement

A special note of thanks goes to our friends, Robin and Rich Wyman – who, for the month of March, 2017 when they were enjoying much needed rest and relaxation in Florida after their first summer and fall of cottage rental exhaustion at their beautiful cottages, Grey Shingles Camps located in Wolfeboro, NH – for their generous offer to me to use their home, whenever I wanted, to finish this book.

Although I have my art studio and many other places in my home where I can write, there are just too many distractions that could prevent me from finishing this book in a timely manner. I was more than happy to water plants, etc., in exchange but they already had someone who would come by to take care of that task for them. And, so, thank you, Robin and Rich, for lending me the use of your home. It was exactly the quiet haven I needed to finish this book.

Seven Storied Houses

You're Out

George sat at the table, sipping his coffee out of a thick white mug. He liked this mug. It reminded him of the mugs they used to serve coffee in at diners, when there were diners. You don't find them around much anymore. People want fancy everything now. He missed the days when life was simple, when you could walk into a diner, find a stool at the counter, and order a cup of coffee. Now you needed to buy breakfast along with that cup of coffee. You're taking up valuable real estate if you're just sitting and sipping a cup of joe. George visited his regular diner, one of the few still open, the last time he took the subway into the city. When he asked for a cup of coffee, they served it in a fragile, thin-handled mug and slid a menu directly behind it. He's always had big hands - hard-working hands - and when he tried to slip his sausage-sized finger into the delicate handle, he knew it would never fit and picked up the mug with one hand, careful not to grasp it too tight for fear it would crumble in his paw.

"Here you go – we have two specials today, eggs benedict and a Spanish omelet. I'll give you a few minutes with the menu," said the big-busted woman with a frosted highlight right down the center of her hair that made George think of a Badger.

"I just want the coffee," George said, politely.

The waitress grabbed the menu and gave George a look and a heavy sigh as if he had just eaten a full-course meal and stiffed her on the tip.

"Well, you'll have to pay extra for another cup of coffee. If you get breakfast you get a bottomless cup. And there are people waiting to sit for breakfast, too." Another exaggerated sigh as she walked away.

George glanced over his shoulder expecting to see a long line at the entrance. There was one middle-aged couple who were being seated at that moment. George felt unwelcome and uncomfortable and decided that, like everything else, the diner dining experience had changed and thought it would be one more thing he would give up.

He didn't have many pleasures anymore. Most of the places he liked to go were either gone or, like the diner, had changed so much he didn't recognize them as the enjoyable places they once were. Or maybe it was the people. People, after all, represent the places where they work. If a waitress or waiter is rude to you in a restaurant, you don't take it out on them, you take it out on the restaurant and won't go there again. And the owner doesn't even know they've lost a patron.

It was at times like this, when he was sitting at his table, sipping a cup of coffee, that he thought about

Carol the most. He couldn't believe that six years had gone by since her passing. And then he would get angry because it just didn't seem fair that only four years after his retirement, Carol got sick. They had so many plans. She wanted to down-size and move to a smaller house in a senior neighborhood, one of those retirement communites. They had talked about Florida but neither of them liked the heat so that wasn't going to happen. But George loved this house where they had raised their two children. They had made so many memories here, like the time Carol's water broke and their oldest, Sandy, who was three at the time, ran to get a bucket to "catch mommy's water, in case the baby needs a drink later." They did make it to the hospital just in time and out popped Jason not ten minutes after getting Carol into the OR. Sandy slept through the whole thing but she says she remembers. He was pretty sure she remembered it only because they had talked about it so many times.

And then there was the time Jason stepped on a nail in the back yard. They were re-doing the porch since the wood had started to rot underneath. The guys who were working on it had left a lot of the old wood, with rusted nails still in it, lying around the yard. George, as usual, was too busy with work so didn't notice until Jason came running into the house, hopping on one foot and screaming bloody murder. They were just getting ready to sit down to dinner and here comes Jason with a piece of rotten board stuck to the bottom of his shoe with the nail stuck in his foot. Screaming. George realized immediately what had happened and grabbed Jason, his keys, and ran out the door to rush to the hospital. George thought about that day now and still wondered how he got there because Jason had screamed the entire time he was in the truck. At seven years old, he had the lungs of an opera singer, hitting the highest notes known to man. But George barely remembered the screaming he was so focused on getting his son to the hospital and getting the nail out of his foot before gangrene set in. He had seen some cases of gangrene when he was in the war. Not a pretty sight. One of his buddies got it really bad and George had strong visuals that would never leave his memory. It became his go-to image when he thought about gangrene.

So, he would ask Carol, how can we possibly leave our home? Of course, this wasn't the same house that they bought forty years ago. It was surprising to George how fast the house deteriorated when it wasn't regularly maintained and either painted or power-washed. The minor repairs he had ignored had turned into major undertakings that would now cost hundreds or thousands of dollars. And now there was so much work that needed to be done on the place, he just didn't have the energy and certainly not the money, either. But sometimes he thought maybe he'd get it painted or at least have the gutters cleaned. Then he would pour himself another cup of coffee and his thoughts would return to Carol.

Maybe if the kids had visited more he would have kept the house up, but since Carol died, he saw them less and less. They both lived out of state and led busy lives working and raising their own families. Of course, the kids were closer to their mom than they were to him. He had worked a lot and so he hadn't been around much, except on weekends. Even then he sometimes had to go in to work on Saturdays for a few hours. But Carol took care of everything in the house, even when they got the estimates to repair their porch. She took care of the cooking and cleaning and raising the kids. He knew he didn't tell her enough how much he appreciated everything she did for the family. When the kids moved away after college and they got married, he and Carol would travel to visit them during holidays. When Carol first got sick the kids had come as often as they could. Then when she got really bad and was in the hospital, they came less often. Once she had passed, their visits pretty much stopped. Sandy called more than Jason but even then it was every few months. George used to call them but seemed to always call at a bad time so he thought it best if he waited until they called him. But they didn't. He tried to understand, remembering his own busy life as a young man supporting a family. They hadn't been back to the house since Carol had passed. He knew it was because it would be too painful for them to come back to their home without their mom there. Then he would feel guilty and think that Carol was right, they should have down-sized. Maybe the kids would visit him if he lived someplace other than the house where they'd grown up. A new place wouldn't have the memories in it for them that this house did. But it was too late now. He wasn't going anywhere.

About a year after Carol died, he decided to get a dog.
He thought that he needed a companion but wasn't
interested in meeting a woman. He had married the
love of his life and no one could replace her. But a
dog would make a good companion. They had one
when the kids were younger but when it died at 12
years old, both of their kids were so upset that they
never got another one. And then not long after that
they went to college. He never thought about it again
until he was sitting one day at the table like he was
now and suddenly thought about getting another dog.
He could use the exercise, too, and thought it would
be good for him to get out and walk. He didn't want a
puppy since the potty training and all that was a lot of
work. He went to the pound and found one that
caught his eye. It was around seven, they told him. Its
owner was sick and couldn't take care of it anymore.
Its name was Buddy. He knew it was an omen and
meant to be since Buddy had been the name of his
dog when he was a kid.

A medium-sized mongrel, a mix of beagle and a
spaniel of some kind, was the perfect companion.
From that moment on, George and Buddy were
inseparable. George took him to visit his friend, Dick
Olsen, when they played chess. Buddy would patiently
lie on the floor near George's feet. He never
complained or begged for anything, appearing content
with George's company. George bought him the best
dog food and would give him some steak mixed in
from time to time. He also bought him a beef bone
but Buddy wasn't interested in chewing hard things.
The vet had said that was OK, dogs usually had a need

to chew more when they were younger. So he bought some baked crunchy dog bones that came in a box that Buddy really liked. But mostly Buddy loved going for walks with George. They also visited another friend of George's, Marvin Johnston. He always had a big beef bone for Buddy even though Buddy never ate them. You could tell though that Buddy appreciated the gesture. He licked Marvin's hand. "See, he likes it, he just said 'Thank you.'" George would wink at Buddy; they had a few private jokes.

But the chess games stopped a couple of years ago when Dick Olsen died and then the beef bones stopped when Marvin went into a nursing home not long after; diabetes had got the better of him. George visited him a couple of times but Marvin was depressed all the time and didn't seem to want any company.

And then a year ago, just like that, Buddy died. George will never forget that day. He got up and dressed to take Buddy for their morning walk. As soon as Buddy heard the leash tinkle with the sound of his ID and rabies vaccination tags, he would come running. This morning he did not. He usually slept in his bed in the kitchen next to the stove, especially in the winter when it got a little chilly at night. In the summer he slept in his bed in George's bedroom. George walked into the kitchen and there was Buddy curled up, looking like he was asleep. But when George walked over to pat his head, he knew immediately that Buddy was gone.

A tear rolled off George's face and fell into his empty mug. He wiped his face with the back of his hand and got up to refill his mug. He poured a little milk into the cup and sitting back down, swirled the coffee slowly, dispersing the milk. He smiled at the white swirl that made him think of Carol. He saw her face, her smile, her curly gray hair. She never liked going gray and was coloring it every four weeks or so and finally got tired of doing it. One day she came to him and announced her decision. He was sitting where he now sat, at the kitchen table, drinking coffee in this very mug, reading the newspaper.

"Well, it's official. From this day forward you will be married to an old lady. What do you think of that?"

George put the paper down and looked at his wife who, to him, could never look like an old lady with her still shapely legs, tight butt, and bright, always-smiling beautiful hazel eyes.

"Are you telling me you want a divorce? Because that's the only way I'd be married to an old lady; if I was married to someone else."

She smiled, turned around, and walked out of the room. Good answer. He wasn't quite sure at the time what the announcement meant but several weeks later he caught her looking closely at her roots in the mirror. After that he again caught her checking the progress of the gray pushing its way down onto the colored golden brown hair. Then one morning he rolled over in bed and there was a curly gray head lying next to him.

Change. Change was what George didn't like. Too many times in his life change meant the end of something, usually something good. And then something else would replace it, usually something bad. George never thought of himself as a negative person; he often would see the good in others even when they didn't see it in themselves. But now, when he took the time to look back at his life, it was change that had become his enemy.

Just like the neighborhood where he lived. Change made it unrecognizable from what it was when he and Carol bought their home nearly fifty years ago now. There was a time when he knew every neighbor on his street. But slowly, one by one, they moved out, to Florida or closer to where their kids and grandkids lived. Now he couldn't even tell you who was living next door. But they were noisy. It was a noisy street. He remembered back in his early married days, Sunday afternoons when everyone was cooking a roast and the smell drifted out the open windows. You could walk by each home and figure out exactly what they were having for dinner. And it was peaceful. People were watching TV or the kids were playing games or reading or a radio was playing Big Band music, like Glenn Miller and Duke Ellington. Now when windows were open mostly it smelled like boiled cabbage or the odor of rotting garbage drifted out into the air. And there was yelling. TV was louder with gun shots and screaming. Even the music was violent. Sometimes when George was walking down the street and he would hear a gun shot from an open window he instinctively ducked. He wasn't sure if it was the

TV or if a bullet was heading his way. The cops were
around a lot, too. He didn't know what people were
doing to each other in their homes but most of them
seemed to have ended up married to the wrong
person.

He shook his head, trying to rattle all these bad
memories out, or wishing only the good ones would
come to him. But the good ones made him sad to
think about since they were all old ones. Come to
think of it, George hadn't had a good anything happen
since he lost Buddy nearly a year ago now. Walks
weren't the same anymore. Before, he had a mission;
Buddy needed the exercise. And it made Buddy really
happy to walk, too. George was walking less and less.
And once the cold came, well, his coat didn't seem to
keep him as warm as it used to so he spent more time
indoors. Some days he barely got out of his chair at
the kitchen table. He swished the coffee in his cup.
Another tear fell in. He raised his arm and wiped his
sleeve across his eyes.

Feeling a little hungry, George went to the fridge to
see what there was to eat. A mostly empty fridge
greeted him with leftover chicken noodle soup still in
the pot, grape jelly, a quart of milk with just enough in
it for one more cup of coffee, a plate with some kind
of meat that had a green tint, yellow mustard, ketchup,
and a shriveled apple. George smiled.

"Yes, I know, I should buy some food. I'm not
hungry anymore, my love. And without you here to
tell me I am, I just don't think about it." George

loved his conversations with Carol. From her grave she was still taking care of him. They didn't talk as much as when she first left him and he missed it. He knew she was right and decided to go to the supermarket to buy a few things. His milk was only going to last for one more cup of coffee and if he didn't have his coffee, well, life just wasn't worth living.

There was a chill in the air and George pulled his worn corduroy jacket tighter to him. He got into his Ford pickup. He loved this old truck. People complained about Ford vehicles, Found On Road Dead, Fix Or Repair Daily, those kinds of things, but George never had any trouble with his truck. Maybe he just got a good one. But he took care of it, too. He didn't have a garage, but it was a tough truck, it didn't need a garage. It could withstand the Massachusetts winters, no problem. And it never got stuck in the snow either. Of course, they used to wrap the tires in chains in winter. But then they came out with all-season radials and Carol insisted they put those on the truck. They worked OK, but not nearly as good as the chains, especially if you got stuck in snow and ice.

George wasn't sure what to buy at the store so got a basket and put in replacements for what he saw in the fridge; whole milk, of course, a couple of cans of chicken noodle soup, a piece of steak, at least he thought that was what he saw in there. He also got a new jar of grape jelly, a loaf of white bread, some Jif peanut butter, and some more Maxwell House coffee. George didn't like the instant. He knew it was faster but it didn't take that much time to brew a cup and besides, he liked a pot of coffee. He didn't always drink the whole pot. He used to make a pot for him and Carol and they would drink the whole pot together, sitting at the table, him reading the paper, her doing crossword puzzles.

That was what they were doing the day she fainted. They were both sitting there, him reading, her doing puzzles, when she slumped over and, spilling her cup of coffee, fell right to the floor. George jumped out of his chair, stared at the coffee running down the plastic-coated table cloth to the floor where it was dripping onto Carol's curly gray head. He grabbed her, frantic, feeling like the time Jason had stepped on the nail, and tried to sit her up.

"Carol! Carol!" He felt her pulse. It was beating. He gently laid her down and grabbed the kitchen phone off the wall. He was glad he had agreed to a cordless phone. Carol wanted it, complaining that she couldn't move around the room when the kids called to talk because the cord couldn't reach. Of course, as usual, she was right and he was grateful, at that moment, that they had the cordless phone. He ran back to Carol as he dialed 911.

"What is your emergency?"

"My wife, she just collapsed. We were sitting at the table, and please, please hurry." He felt tears in his eyes and quickly gave his address.

"We'll be there as soon as we can. Is she still breathing?"

"Yes."

"OK, that's good. Why don't you stay on the line with us until the ambulance gets there."

"OK." George held the phone as if Carol's life depended on it. He held it as tight as he could without cracking the plastic in his hands. With the other arm he held Carol's head, cradling her against his chest.

"Stay with me, my love. Don't leave me, please don't leave me." That was all he could say, over and over.

It seemed to take hours before the ambulance got there but he knew it was just minutes. They lived fairly close to St. Beth's Memorial Hospital. They lived close to every type of store or business they would possibly ever need which was why they had bought the house. The schools, the shopping center, the hospital, everything one wants close by when raising a family. It was a good choice.

Cancer. That was what the doctors said. Brain cancer to be exact. But where does it come from? That was the question on George's lips. People smoke and they get lung cancer. They drink too much they might get liver cancer. They don't eat well and some other cancer sprouts somewhere in their stomach or other internal organ. But how do you protect yourself against getting brain cancer? George couldn't figure it out and wondered what it meant for Carol. What was she going to have to go through to get well because as far as he was concerned, there was no other option. Surgery, the doctors said, to try to remove all the cancer. So she had surgery. He visited her in the hospital with her head wrapped as if she had just washed her hair; except she was so pale. She insisted on wearing lipstick and wouldn't have any visitors without putting some color on her lips. She would even pinch her cheeks to try to make herself look healthy. Imagine that, George thought, she was battling the big 'C' and she was concerned about the people visiting her. She wanted to look her best, for them.

She came home. They thought they got all the cancer. But a month later, when she went back for a checkup, the cancer was now in her lymph nodes. It was very aggressive. She was back in the hospital within two months after the surgery and passed away, surrounded by George, Jason, and Sandy, quietly and without fanfare. George held her hand when she took her last breath. She had been in a coma for about two days. They said it wouldn't take long. They were right. He had called the children and they had come immediately.

Carol wanted to be cremated so that was what they did. Her urn sits on the mantle in their home. Sandy will take it when George passes away and she'll take George's ashes, too. Jason tried to make a stink saying he didn't want to be left out but George silenced him with a look and said in his stern voice - the one that always meant to Jason, I mean business - "No one is going to separate me from your mother." Jason nodded; he understood. His parents were deeply in love, had always been, and would never be separated, even in death.

George found his way to the cashier. He went to the 10 items or less register and the cashier checked him out without looking at him. George looked at her the entire time; he had gone to her register many times before. He waited for her to look up so he could say hello. She didn't seem to recognize him.

"That's $23.82." He handed her $30. She gave him the change, still without looking.

"Thank you and you have a nice day." She was already ringing up the next person before George had even put his change away.

"Thank you." George took his two bags and slowly walked to his truck in the parking lot.

When he got home, he put the items away and made himself a pot of coffee. Coffee was one of the few pleasures in life that he still enjoyed. To just sit and drink a cup, that was pure pleasure. Just the smell of it brewing made him salivate. He imagined he had an addiction to coffee, if there was such a thing. He was pretty sure there was since he saw on the *Today* show something about caffeine addiction. He listened to what they said and although he never believes they are talking about him, as he sat here now sipping his coffee he remembered that segment and thought he must be a caffeine addict since he loved coffee and drank so much of it every day. Not having any side effects from the coffee, it was difficult for him to think about having an addiction. But if it was like alcohol or drugs or even gambling, an addiction was something you thought about all the time and had to have. Yeah, that was him. He thought about coffee a lot and drank it a lot.

"Son of a bitch." George shook his head at his inability to recognize sooner this weakness in himself. Even though he loved coffee, the taste, the smell, everything about it, he never thought of himself as having an addictive personality. He could let anything go if he thought it had too great of a hold on him. In other words, if he felt he might be out of control. If it was alcohol he would have quit drinking, just like that. He tried smoking when he was young but it made him cough and his eyes burn. That was enough for him to know that this was not a good thing. And he quit, just like that.

"I am a little hungry, now that I think about it. I will, I'll eat a little something. You don't need to worry about me." His frequent conversations with Carol were usually about his health. He chuckled to himself. Thinking about addictions made him think about Carol. If anything or anyone had a hold on him, it was her. She was very likely the only person or thing that he gave in to completely. He was hers and she was his. He used to tell her, "Who needs alcohol or cigarettes when I have my Carol. You are my addiction." She would blush and giggle as he planted a big kiss on her cheek, hugging her with his strong hairy arms, touching her face with his rough calloused hands. When he held her he often felt like he had a tiny Chickadee in his hands. Not that Carol was so small and fragile. George always thought she was just right; not too skinny and not fat. But underneath her tough exterior he knew she had vulnerabilities. He knew she needed his big shoulders to lean on and his warm comforting arms to love and protect her. He was her rock; there was no doubt about it.

George opened a can of soup and poured it into a small pot adding a cup of water to the pot. He stirred the soup and started to reach for a bowl but stopped. He decided to eat the soup right out of the pot. Why dirty a bowl when the pot was all he needed. For the longest time he automatically grabbed two bowls. Then he would reach for two bowls and stop himself. Then he would grab just one bowl. Now, he usually just ate right out of the pot. If he had leftovers he just put the pot right into the refrigerator and would reheat it the next day. He poured himself another cup of coffee and sat back down at the kitchen table.

Days like this he thought about watching a little TV. Occasionally he would watch a basketball game but mostly he just sat and thought about Carol and the kids when they were young. He had so many memories that entertained him and meant so much more to him than any TV program ever could. He recalled the Thanksgiving when Carol burnt their turkey so badly that they had to go out to dinner. And they were having company, too, so George ended up buying dinner for his parents and his sister and brother-in-law. The kids were both pretty young so they could split a plate. But he called that their 'most expensive Thanksgiving dinner.' Then there was the time the kids tried to make them a Christmas present – Sandy was eight and Jason was five. Or were they nine and six? No, he was pretty sure they were eight and five. They wanted to do something really special for mommy and daddy. They decided to bake a cake. Mommy was concerned when they said they needed to use the oven but didn't want to discourage them from creating their 'surprise' gift. They didn't tell her they were baking a cake. Sandy spent a lot of time around her mom when Carol was cooking and baking in the kitchen so Sandy was pretty confident she knew what she was doing. It was the worst most misshapen blob of mess they had ever seen. And both George and Carol ate a piece with Sandy and Jason crying the entire time. The good news was, Sandy developed a new respect for her mother's cooking and baking skills and really paid attention after that. It was a humbling experience for the eight-year-old. Or was she nine?

So many memories. Most of them really good. A few not so good, but the good far outweighed the bad. He and Carol rarely fought and they mostly agreed on child-rearing. And they just seemed to know what each other needed. There was only one time that George could recall when he was completely confused about what was going on with Carol: the change. She was hot, she was cold, she was angry, she was emotional and crying. He didn't know how to help her and as she reminded him time and time again, "You can't help me so stop trying!" It was George's job to fix things, to make things right. But this he could not fix. It only lasted a couple of years and then they were back to normal. She was still hot and cold and angry and emotional sometimes but far less than she had been during those two years.

George noticed his soup was bubbling to the top of the pot and jumped up to turn off the burner. He decided to let the pot cool off a bit before he brought it back to the table. He grabbed a pot holder off the side of the stove that was held on by a magnet sewn into the top. He put it on the table and after a few minutes he brought the pot over to the table. Chicken noodle, although his favorite, was losing its appeal. He took three or four bites and returned the pot to the stove.

George sipped his coffee and when he went to refill his cup, noticed the pot was empty. He unplugged the coffee pot and almost automatically set about making a fresh pot. But he checked the clock and noticed it was 10:45. So he washed the pot out, filled it with water and the basket with fresh coffee, and put it into the percolator, ready for tomorrow morning.

He shuffled his way to the bedroom, turning the nightstand light on. He still slept on his side of the bed, still said good-night to Carol every single night, and still kissed her framed photo on his nightstand every single night, too. George lay down on the bed and stared up at the ceiling. He thought about Carol lying next to him. He thought about Buddy who gave him so much comfort when Carol had gone. He still kept Buddy's bed at the foot of the bed. The clock read 11:12. He wasn't the least bit tired but he felt more exhausted than he'd ever felt before. He was restless but he also had no energy. He felt weary with an aching in his bones that would not let him sleep. He knew what he had to do.

Carol's morphine sat on the shelf in the bathroom medicine cabinet exactly where it had been when she was still alive. Although she only used it a couple of times when the pain had been so bad, there was nearly a full bottle left. George wasn't sure how long medications lasted past their expiration date but thought they were probably still potent enough. He took the bottle, filled a glass with water, and went back to his bedroom.

George opened the bottle and dumped the contents into his hand. There was no hesitation as he took the first pill and sipped the water. Then he took another and another until the handful of pills was gone. He put the bottle on his nightstand and held the glass in one hand and Carol's photo in the other hand. George smiled at the face staring back at him. As he raised her photo to his lips, a tear ran down his cheek and fell into the empty glass. George put the glass down and lay back on the bed, placing the photo on the pillow next to him.

"Good night, Carol, my love."

Seven Storied Houses

Settling

Gordon and Helen Whiting lived a quiet life in a neighborhood that was a reflection of their existence and everything they represented. The Whitings, retired for several years, shopped at the local supermarket on Tuesdays, drove to church together on Sundays, and had eaten breakfast at Betty's Homestyle Cooking Restaurant after church - every Sunday - for 11 years. Helen got her hair washed and set every week, on Thursdays at 2pm, as she had done for going on 25 years. Gordon went to the Elks Lodge on Saturdays to smoke a cigar and have a glass of brandy with other retired men in the neighborhood. He and Jim Duncan, a neighbor he golfed with in the summer, often went to the Elks club together. Helen played Mahjong with four other retired women in the neighborhood on Fridays at 11am. The hostess provided a light lunch of cucumber or olive loaf sandwiches, a slice of apple or cherry pie, and a glass of sherry.

The Whitings were quite satisfied with their lives and felt blessed for the good friends and neighbors they had. With no children or grandchildren to talk to or care for, they had always come and gone as they pleased, taking a vacation now and then to places they either had never been before or more often going to the same places year after year. They were creatures of habit and didn't stray too far from their comfort zones.

A member of Rotary, Gordon was connected with several overseas locations where they stayed in luxury while abject poverty lived outside their window. It wasn't so much that they believed they were above the people who served them, or cleaned their rooms in the hotels where they stayed, or who begged on the streets outside their windows, but they felt that this was the way of life, the nature of things, and how life was different for those who have much and for those who have nothing.

Of course, they gave donations when they could; they had a few favorite charities that they gave to yearly. Gordon provided them with a solid, comfortable retirement where they would never want for anything. Helen had worked for a while when they first married but Gordon liked having her at home.

Earlier in their relationship they were more spontaneous and would go off to the beach when he got home from work. When she was working she was often too tired or had to get up early for work so couldn't stay out late at night. She liked her job but it was demanding. Sometimes she even had to bring work home over the weekends. She worked for a small office and, as the main bookkeeper, she just couldn't get it all done in a day. They really needed to hire another bookkeeper but as long as she continued to do the work, there was no incentive for them to hire more help. That was when Gordon came up with the brilliant idea to hire her; Helen could work for him by keeping their finances straight. He never liked taking care of the bills anyway but felt it was his job since Helen dealt with payables and receivables all day long. But with her experience, he thought it was a perfect solution. So Helen quit her job when she was 26 and worked for Gordon running their household finances. And he gave her a weekly paycheck.

They complemented each other rather nicely. Amiable and cordial, they fit together like a pair of well-worn gloves.

"We're a couple of old slippers, that's what we are." Gordon loved describing their marriage this way.

"Yes sir, comfortably worn, that's it. Or you're the holey sock and I'm the worn slipper. Or maybe I'm the sweater with the ragged elbows and you're the patches. No, I like the slipper and holey sock better, don't you?"

Helen didn't like any of it. She didn't like being worn or holey or an old anything. She lifted weights, not heavy but enough to keep her toned. And she did the stair climber to keep her stomach flat. She liked feeling strong and in shape. She didn't dress like a lot of the older women in the neighborhood but more like someone half her age. She knew that sometimes when she went to play Mahjong they would snicker when she showed up wearing her skinny jeans. But she didn't care what they thought of her. Not anymore. She was bored, bored with the same old thing, bored with her comfortable life. Bored with the emptiness she felt inside when she sat at the Mahjong table sipping sherry and eating yet another slice of apple pie. Bored as her hairdresser rattled on about her abusive boyfriend and how this time he meant it, he wouldn't hit her again because he really loved her and their two-year-old son. He didn't want to lose them. Helen couldn't stand any of it anymore. She wanted to yell at Rachel, "He won't stop, abusers never do, and if you keep taking him back he will lose you, permanently, when he kills you!" She wanted to set fire to Betty's Homestyle Cooking Restaurant so that they would have to go someplace new, just once. And the closer she got to 60, the more she wanted to throw open the windows in their Architectural Digest designed home and scream to those within earshot of her front window, "I'm mad as hell and I'm not going to take it anymore!"

Her life was a lie. She knew it but she was helpless to do anything about it. She gave her life to Gordon over thirty years ago. And now, at 56, she was stuck. How could she leave this marriage? She couldn't survive in the style she had become accustomed to on the paycheck she received from Gordon each month. And if she left him that paycheck would end. She would have to find an apartment and a job paying more than minimum wage. Because even though she worked on their finances for over 30 years it wasn't the same as working for a company and she most likely would have to start at the bottom. At 56 years old. She couldn't see herself doing that. But she also wondered what holding this lie inside her was doing to her physically and mentally.

So she made the decision, several years ago, that she would accept her fate, keep quiet, and live a comfortable but unfulfilled life. When she first had these thoughts, in her mid-40's, it was a little late to start saving her own money separate from the household money, just in case she got the courage to actually up and leave this idyllic life. But, she did put some money away anyway and now she had a small stash even though she knew it wouldn't be enough to live on for more than a couple of years. If she got a job, she could maybe stretch the savings out a few more years but she would need to scrimp on everything. No more weekly hair appointments, no exotic vacations, no weekly Mahjong with the ladies. Well, she would willingly give up Mahjong – that hadn't made her life any more fulfilling. And go back to cleaning her own toilet? She hadn't had to do that for more years than she could count now. No more gorgeous home with the latest appliances, no Egyptian cotton sheets, no Laura Ashley window treatments, and certainly no Stearns and Foster mattress. She would definitely have to surrender her Lord and Taylor and Nordstrom credit cards and go back to bargain basement shopping.

She cringed when she thought about the life she lived before meeting Gordon. She had actually used a cable spool as a coffee table in her living room. The table cloth she put over it, although hiding its true colors, couldn't hide the truth of what was underneath. It represented poverty and everything she hated about her life growing up. There was no doubt she loved all the material things about her life now. But she wondered, more than once, were these things enough?

And then there was Gordon. What about Gordon? Did she love him? Well, sure, at least as much as you can love someone you've spent more than half of your life with. Why spend that much time with them if you *don't* love them? The old slipper and the holey sock. She hated that, so why didn't she just tell Gordon?

A good man, Gordon was a creature of habit. At fourteen years older than Helen, he wasn't about to change much either. He loved their routines as much as Helen hated them. He was always faithful to her, she was positive about that. He loved his wife. She loved Gordon. She just wasn't in love with Gordon. Not anymore. Time changes everything. The passion dwindles. The love becomes a routine; a peck on the cheek, an occasional hug, a touch of the arm. Just another thing we do along with brewing the coffee, brushing our teeth, and putting on a clean pair of socks. Socks. She kept a pair of holey socks and a ripped t-shirt she owned before she and Gordon had started dating. Just as a reminder. She didn't want to ever forget where she came from and what kind of life she had lived. She found the old socks and t-shirt many years later at the bottom of a drawer. She realized then that she didn't have to keep them as a reminder because she would never forget. When you are unable to take care of your basic needs, that kind

of thing gets under your skin like a splinter. You can't
wash it off as you would a temporary tattoo. It is
there forever, a reminder like the time you fell off your
bike and slashed your knee on a piece of broken glass.
It leaves a scar and every time you look at that scar
you recall the fall, the blood, the stitches.

Over the years she would try to mix things up a little;
suggest a new location for vacation, a new restaurant
for breakfast, a new hobby they could do together.
And they would try these different things for a short
time. And then, within weeks, and sometimes after
trying this new hobby only once, they were back to the
same old routines; back to Mahjong and Sherry for
Helen and back to the Elks lodge, a cigar, and Brandy
for Gordon.

But one of the changes Gordon agreed to make did
stick. They decided to host a foreign exchange
student for a month. They did it a few years in a row
and actually enjoyed it. If it was a boy, Gordon would
take him golfing and to his lodge. If a girl stayed with
them Helen was in charge and got to take her
shopping, the hairdressers, and to see a movie (often
one that she knew Gordon wouldn't like.) The
student, usually a senior in high school, could speak
some English at least, and often very good English. It
was like having a taste of what it would be like to have
a child or a grandchild of their own. Helen, in
particular, loved having a young person around. It
immediately made her feel younger and it seemed as if
any aches and pains she may have had just melted
away, at least while the student was staying with them.

When the month was over, the student would go on
to live with another host family and Gordon and
Helen Whiting would return to their regularly
scheduled lives.

Amado Torres arrived from the Philippines and
Gordon and Helen were at the airport to meet him.
Gordon held up a sign with Amado's name on it.
Helen was looking for a small boy – stereotypes told
her the Filipinos were a small people – which would
explain how they both looked right past the tall,
handsome young man standing right in front of them.

"Amado?" Helen was the first to see him. "Are you
Amado?"

"Hello, yes, I am Amado."

Gordon snapped out of his reverie and turned to look
at the young man who was holding Helen's hand.
They both stared at the brown Adonis like he
materialized out of thin air right before their eyes.
Gordon looked around to see if anyone else could see
him. Helen couldn't take her eyes off him and
continued to stare at him while he seemed unable to
let go, held fast by her eyes. They shared a moment.

"Gordon here." Gordon extended a hand and Amado
let go of Helen's. Helen looked at her hand and then
at Amado. She put her hands on her hips, smiling,
watching Amado's lips as he answered the simple,
routine questions that Gordon threw at him. A smile,
a blush, his eyes, deep and delicious, back to Helen,
smiling, blushing, back to Gordon.

"So, let's get your bags and get out of here. Are you hungry, son?"

Son. Oh my God, what am I thinking? Helen almost said out loud what was in her mind. This, this boy, could be her *son*. No, her *grandson*, almost. Yes, almost her grandson. Her face felt hot. She knew she was feeling inappropriately, not at all as someone who is old enough to be a grandmother. She felt sick.

Back at the house Helen brought Amado to the guest room.

"I'll let you get settled, OK? If you need anything just let me know. You can put your clothes in the dresser there or hang up some clothes in the closet. I'll be around the house. Gordon can show you the place. Dinner will be at 6:30 but maybe you want to wash up? Towels are in the bathroom right through that door." Helen stood in the doorway and pointed to the dresser, the closet, and the bathroom door.

"Thank you so much, Madam. I am most grateful." Amado bowed ever so slightly and when he looked up, he was smiling, flashing his perfect teeth.

"Oh please, call me Helen." And Helen walked away, closing the door behind her.

The days passed quietly. Amado spent weekdays at the high school and was dropped off at their home after classes each day. He was very athletic and participated in many of the sports the school had to offer. His favorite was soccer, which he played in the

Philippines. Every team at the school wanted him on theirs. He was smart, too. Excelling in everything he did, he couldn't have been more perfect.

One night after dinner, Gordon was itching to go to his club. He asked Amado if he wanted to go with him but Amado, who was napping after dinner, declined the offer. He had some studying he wanted to do for school. His goal was to learn as much as he could about America for the year he was in this country. Gordon admired the boy's ambition and gave Amado a thumbs-up.

"Good boy! You'll do well in life. Hard work, that's what it takes."

Helen retired to the living room and picked up a book she had been reading, a Pulitzer winner. She had decided that since she was a slow reader, she wouldn't waste her time reading bad writing. If she was going to read, and she loved to read, she was going to read the Pulitzers. Since she made this decision about three years ago, she had only read about five of the winners. This one, "The Brief Wondrous Life of Oscar Wao" was a little more challenging. Spanish words were written throughout so she had to stop her reading and look up a word or two before she could go on. She felt like she was missing too much if she ignored the Spanish words. She was deep into Chapter 3 when she realized Amado was standing in front of her.

"Oh, hi Amado, can I help you with something?" She blushed at his closeness and their aloneness. He seemed to be thinking about what he wanted to say.

"May I sit?"

Helen, who had her legs curled up on the couch, put her feet down on the floor.

"Certainly, sit, please."

"First I want to thank you so much for all you and Mr. Whiting, Gordon, have done for me these past few weeks. It has been truly a dream for me."

Helen felt her skin getting warm. She still couldn't believe this young man had that effect on her.

"Well, Amado, it is our pleasure. I'm so happy we can do this for you."

Helen could tell he wanted to say more. He kept his head down. She put her book down and leaned towards him.

"Yes, Amado, what is it?"

"Mrs. Whiting… Helen…" he reached for her hand that was on the sofa. She felt her hand go limp and let him pick it up, bring it to his lips and kiss it ever so softly with lips, slightly parted, applying the smallest bit of pressure. As he pulled his lips away, she felt him breathe in her scent. She knew the right thing to do was to pull her hand away but she wanted to play this out, see where he would go with this. Was this a young man who was ever so grateful for their kindnesses or something more?

"I must tell you, I believe I am in love with you."

Helen quickly pulled her hand away.

"Oh, no, Amado, that isn't possible, I am way too old for you. You are just grateful, that's all, and I am so happy that you are, really... I..."

He slid in close to her and taking her face in his hands, pulled her lips to his. A tingling ran down her neck, rested briefly on her nipples, and then headed straight for the highly neglected area between her legs. She let him hold her to him for what seemed like an hour but she knew couldn't have been more than thirty seconds. And then she pulled away.

"Amado, I don't think you should be..."

"I am sorry... Helen... for what I feel for you. I don't know if this is wrong when it feels so right. I would love for you to come to bed with me so I can pleasure you."

She sighed. A longing inside her made her quiver with excitement. Her body was screaming, yes, go, be with him for just this one time. Reason stopped her and she tried ever so hard to clear her head.

"Amado, I am so flattered that you want to do this... for me... but... it isn't right. We don't do things that way here, in this country."

"You don't give each other pleasure when you feel love and desire?"

"No, no that isn't what I'm saying. I'm married and I'm so much older than you, I could be your gran… your mother and it just isn't right."

"When I first met you at the airport, I felt it when I touched your hand. And I think you did, too. I saw it in your face, your eyes. It has been so difficult being here with you, feeling these feelings for you and not being able to touch you. But I'm leaving to go with the other family in just a few days and I had to share my feelings for you."

"Amado, you have your whole life before you. I don't know how much time I have, how many more years. You will meet a young woman and get married. A woman you can share your life with and grow old together." As Helen said all this she imagined that she was this young woman; that she was starting her life over with Amado, a new life, with a man so loving and handsome. A man who kissed like Amado kissed. Who made her tingle, a sensation she hadn't felt in so many years. She wanted to be that woman.

She knew she could never be that woman.

"I think you should go to your room, Amado, and we should not speak about this again. I do want you to know how flattered I am but this just is not possible. You are a very special man. I wish you only the best in your life."

"I will do as you wish, Helen. But know that you are breaking my heart. I will never forget you."

Helen knew there would be many more broken hearts in Amado's life and most likely they would not be his.

Several days later Amado was gone. And less than a week later, so was Helen.

Seven Storied Houses

Alone Together

Apartment 1A

Ben hated working the night-shift. Since he was always the last hired, he always got the worst shift, the one no one else wanted. These were the shifts everyone was eager to get promoted out of and that only happened when there was a new hire which, coincidentally, was usually Ben. Seems he just couldn't stay around long enough to climb to the next level. It didn't matter to Ben where he worked. To him, all manufacturing jobs were the same: candy, furniture, cleaning products, toys, carpeting, even drugs. You name it, Ben had worked there. He had moved so many times he lost count. Twice-divorced, he always told his ex-wives he was a gypsy at heart and couldn't settle down in one place too long.

"I get bored. You know me. And if you don't know me, well, now you do, this is who I am, sweetheart. Get used to it or get lost."

His first wife, Ginny, really fell for him. She stayed the longest, almost eight years. Ben told her up front he wasn't cut out to be a dad and she was 'OK' with that. She had a job she really liked at the Super Food store and didn't want to up and leave when, after five years, Ben was getting itchy. But she did. And after three years of roaming around New Jersey, unable to find work because he couldn't find a job he liked, she finally had it and moved back to her old job in Maine. By the time she left, Ben didn't care anymore and knew that, like every other woman in his life, she would have eventually left anyway.

He met Karla in Jersey when he was ready to head for Ohio. She was excited about traveling and thought she was hooking up with a big spender. They married after knowing each other only about a month and once in Ohio, the same pattern revealed itself. Karla didn't even look for a job. She sat in their sparsely furnished apartment watching soaps and eating bags of chips and ring dings. She gained 25 pounds in the six months they were together. On the same day Ben quit his job at a carpet manufacturing company, he packed his bags and walked out the door leaving Karla with the overdue rent bill.

Boston was Ben's old stomping grounds. He contacted his friends from Revere and Salem. Tommy Flaherty got him a job at GE. He liked assembly line work the most even though robots were replacing a lot of these jobs. The apartment was courtesy of Mikey Johnson who was moving out to live with his girlfriend in an apartment they found in East Boston. They were saving for marriage and a house so it made sense to move in together. Ben was pretty happy with his current situation but missed having regular sex. He thought about going to a bar to pick someone up for the night but knew it would lead to complications or worse; another marriage that would soon end in divorce.

At 7:30pm Ben switched off the TV, turned off the kitchen light, and walked out the door. He had a feeling this job was going to be different. This job would be the one he would stay with. This time.

Apartment 2A

Martha and Jacob Switzer sat in front of the TV watching their favorite show, Wheel of Fortune. Every night at 7pm, no matter what they were doing, they would set up the TV trays with their bowls of chicken and rice soup and saltine crackers, crunched up into the soup, and watch Wheel. They had been doing this, in this very apartment, for the last 17 years. That was when they had down-sized from their large two-story home to the apartment.

Their son, a friend of the building owner, had found the place for them. They were very happy here. The other neighbors were mostly quiet, no loud parties, which suited the Switzer's just fine. They did have a young man who liked to party living in the apartment above them for a short time. That was many years ago now. They complained to their son who kept forgetting to tell his friend, the building owner. When he finally did tell him it took his friend a couple of months before he finally talked to the young man. In the meantime, the Switzer's were forced to take action themselves and would use a broom handle to tap the ceiling, hoping the young man would turn down the stereo or end his party earlier than the usual 1am. After six months or more, when the building owner finally talked with the young man, the noise ended when he moved out a couple of weeks later. But this was the only incident in 17 years. They felt very fortunate.

"How's the soup?" Jacob stopped mid-sip and turned to Martha. His wife, the mother of his children, the love of his life asked the same question every night. And every night he gave the same answer.

"It's fine, dear, just fine. My favorite, you know."

"Yes, I know. Would you like some more saltines?"

"No, I have enough. Just the right amount."

They both turned back to the TV. When they finished eating their soup and Wheel was over they usually watched Jeopardy. Martha got up and brought their bowls into the kitchen. She put the water on for tea.

"How about a couple of Fig Newtons, J? And a cup of tea?" Martha liked to call Jacob 'J', like he was a young man and had a cool nickname. He liked it, too.

"You know I like Fig Newtons."

"How many and what kind of tea do you want?"

"How about a glass of milk instead?"

"Sure. I'm having tea. How many Fig Newtons?"

"I'll have two. That should be plenty."

"Coming right up." Martha got a small plate and put two Fig Newtons on the plate for Jacob and two for her. She shuffled back into the living room and put the Fig Newtons on Jacob's TV tray.

"I just want two." He looked at the plate with the four cookies and wondered if Martha was losing her hearing.

"Why did you give me four?" Martha, in the kitchen pouring Jacob's milk and her mug of tea, shook her head.

"J, two of them are for me and two for you. I just put them all on one plate. Is that OK?"

"Oh, yeah, sure, that's fine." Jacob turned his focus back to the TV where the contestants on Jeopardy were being introduced.

Martha came back into the living room, carrying her mug of tea and Jacob's milk. She put Jacob's milk on his tray and took two of the cookies. She sat on the couch next to Jacob and put her tea on her TV tray and ate her Fig Newton cookies, sipping her tea. Just like every night.

Apartment 5A

Penny lay down on the couch, slipped off her shoes, and put her feet up. Daniel sat on the floor watching his favorite TV show, Daniel Tiger's Neighborhood. He loved that there was a TV show with his name in it. And at four-years-old, it didn't really take much to entertain and delight Danny. Penny was happy to have a moment to rest. Danny was so easy to care for and she appreciated him every day. Working two jobs was exhausting and at the end of the day, she just didn't have much to give to the boy.

She felt herself drifting off to sleep but had to get up to make some dinner. It was almost 7pm and although he didn't complain, she figured the boy had to be hungry since he hadn't eaten since lunch time at daycare. This was another thing she felt lucky about, that she found a reputable day care so close to where they lived. And they accommodated her by allowing her to drop Danny off at 7am, which was a little earlier than most parents dropped their preschoolers off. She had to be at her first job, cleaning rooms at the motel chain, Take Two, at 7:30 where she worked until 11:30. She had a 20 minute drive to her second job as a cashier at Wayside Mart where she worked from noon to 6. She usually snacked on a hotdog or other non-nutritious item in the car on the way to the Mart. Then she picked Danny up and was home most nights by 6:30. She tried her best to make something delicious and nutritious for dinner since she was sure they both needed it. Although the daycare gave Danny his lunch, she was pretty sure he was choking down something similar to what she was eating for lunch.

"Are you hungry, baby?"

"Yes, mommy, I am. Can I help you?" How did she ever get so lucky, she wondered? With a dad who was so delinquent in his child support payments and couldn't take time to visit his son ever, she just didn't know who her little Danny took after.

Having an alcoholic dad and a mom who worked day and night, Penny wondered what she was like as a child and if she was this sweet when she was a little girl. She couldn't remember. There was a lot of crying and fear from having a drunken father. She spent most of her time in her room avoiding him. She didn't know if he would throw up or throw a plate. His behavior was so erratic. He hated that his wife worked so much and Penny couldn't agree more. She needed her mom but knew she was working. Whether she worked so much to pay the bills or worked to get away from her husband, Penny never knew. But she did know that she didn't like being alone so much. Being with her dad, even though he was always there every night, was like being alone. Most nights he fell asleep on the couch with the TV on. If Penny went in to change the channel he would wake up and grumble, "Let it alone! Go to bed, child." She wasn't even sure he knew her name.

Like her mother, Penny had left her husband. Her mom knew she had to get away from the man who was Penny's father in name only. Penny always cried when her mom came home she was so happy to see her, running to her and jumping into her arms. Her father did nothing to care for her, not even feeding her so she was hungry when her mom came home. If her dad woke up he would yell at her mom, accusing her of cheating on him. This went on for a few months before her mom left. It wasn't so bad at first, he was drunk just occasionally, then it became nightly and he lost his job.

"The drink is poison to him. It's a disease. He can't handle it." Her mom tried her best to explain why they were leaving him. Penny didn't care why they were leaving. All she cared about was that they *were* leaving. They moved in with her mom's sister, Cathy, her husband Ryan and their son Donnie who was a year older than Penny and went to Kindergarten. They fixed up the basement for them and Penny was so happy there. They had a little TV downstairs and she could watch whatever she wanted. Donny had a lot of books that she could look at; all his toys were downstairs, too. Penny would have been happy to stay there forever. They slept on a sofa bed and there were a couple of chairs and a small table where they ate their meals. They had a small refrigerator for necessities and a bureau for their clothes. Penny didn't think they needed anything else. But her mom didn't like to impose and had found them an apartment within a few months. It was just a few blocks from her sister's house so they visited them often.

Penny sometimes felt like she was repeating history, except that she didn't have a sister close by to live with and she had to do it all on her own. She had spent many nights looking for apartments in the paper and Sundays driving around looking at them until she found the one they now lived in, which was pretty good and close to everything. Her ex, she heard, had a new girlfriend and a swanky apartment. She had money. Penny wasn't sure if this was true and she didn't much care. All she knew was that their son, Danny, wasn't seeing any of the money.

She cooked the elbow pasta and opened a jar of Ragu spaghetti sauce. Danny liked pasta so they had it a couple of times a week. She knew they both needed some protein at least once a day and tried to have eggs or peanut butter for breakfast. After dinner they watched a little TV together and at 8pm she put Danny to bed. He never complained. It was as if he knew how hard his mother worked and didn't want to make her life any more difficult than it already was. With his jammies on, he climbed into bed.

"Did you brush your teeth, sweetie?"

"Yes, mommy."

"Who's my best boy?"

"Danny!"

"Mommy loves her Danny. Sleep tight."

"Don't let the bed bugs bite!"

Penny turned out his light and made herself comfortable on the couch to watch a little TV before going to bed. Within five minutes she was fast asleep.

Apartment 8A

The alarm went off at the usual time, 6:15am. But at this point she really didn't need it anymore. Getting up early had become a habit, just like when she worked full-time. She used to think they would sleep in on weekends, her and Tony, but she always woke up early. Tony knew how to do it, he knew how to relax and sleep in most days. He only got up early to golf during the season and always slept in during the winter months. And then one morning he just didn't get up. She remembered hearing people say that they wanted to go in their sleep and that was how her Tony went. It was definitely not the way she would have chosen he leave her. And it was terrifying the morning she went in the bedroom with a cup of coffee and when she reached over to caress his face, dropped the cup on the bed when she found a cold hard corpse where the warm soft husband lay just hours before.

Stella's life went on. Her schedule was full each day. She liked being busy. All of her friends were just as busy with classes and doctor appointments. Several of them were empty nesters and living alone in an apartment as she was now. They were there for each other, supported each other, and she was just a phone call away from help if she needed it. She thought about moving to a senior development but to her it was like moving to a nursing home and she felt she still had a lot of life in her. At 77, she wasn't ready to give up and sit looking out a window in a single room with people all around her dying off. She knew she was lucky that she still had her health which made this life possible. Of course her three kids all thought she would be 'happier' in a senior development. But she had so many friends around here it just didn't make sense for her, at this point, to up and leave all of them.

"I'll move into one of those old-people homes when I can't wipe myself, I promise. Is it a deal?" That usually shut the kids up and put smiles on their faces, too.

"It's a deal." Tony Jr., the spokesperson for the three of them, and the oldest of her kids, turned to the others, not expecting any disagreement with their mom's plan.

"Good, then let's not talk about it anymore today. Who wants ice cream?" The grandkids, Zach, Emma, and Scott, would run to the kitchen looking for their bowls with chocolate chip ice cream in them. Although the apartment was small, it was close to where she and Tony had lived and she still loved having the family over like in the old days when they had Thanksgiving in their dining room. Tony Jr. and her youngest, Megan, usually brought a couple of folding chairs so everyone had a chair to sit on and the kids sat on pillows on the floor, which was more fun for them. Only her middle child was still not married and Stella would not relax until Stephanie was 'settled' as she liked to call it. A high-powered corporate woman, Stephanie lived in the city in a fancy apartment. She seemed quite content with her life but Stella felt she knew best for the girl. She tried not to meddle in her kids' lives and would only ask Stephanie how city life was going. Stephanie knew not to reveal too much to her mom and would answer with a simple 'good' that usually put an end to the conversation.

A more nervous driver now, Stella would usually let her younger friends drive them out to lunch or the senior center in town. She would drive in the daytime if she needed to make a run to the convenience store if she was out of creamer or bread. But she didn't do very much alone since she was involved in so many activities. And since many of her friends were younger than her, she always had others who were willing to drive.

Stella was quite content with her life. She talked to Tony every day, keeping him up-to-date on her activities. She never thought about another man or having anyone else that close to her again. "I had the love-of-my-life, I don't need another man." Her kids actually tried fixing her up a couple of times. She did enjoy a nice dinner out with a man and enjoyed the conversation, but she realized these men were just looking for a woman 'to take care of them', which translated to mommy doing their cooking and cleaning. She had had enough of that and preferred to spend time doing the things she enjoyed doing now. She spent far less time cleaning up after herself than she would if she had another man in the house.

She did sometimes feel the ache of no longer having
sex. And she came close to inviting one man into her
bed but decided at the last minute that, looking at the
signs he had been giving her, he was just like all the
rest who wanted a live-in maid. It just wasn't worth it
to her. So, she kept busy and took care of her own
business. She did become quite comfortable with her
vibrator although sometimes an orgasm would bring
images of Tony into her head and she would end up
fetal-positioned and in tears. She thought they would
grow old together and never figured she would grow
old without him.

Stella showered and after a quick breakfast of oatmeal
with raisins and soy milk, a cup of coffee, and her
vitamins, she walked to her friend Sybil's house and
they drove together to the mall. They had a busy day
planned which included shopping at TJ Maxx for a
couple of spring tops, taking a workshop on making
greeting cards, having lunch, and visiting with two
other friends for cocktails and maybe a light dinner.
They talked about watching a movie, *Crazy, Stupid,
Love*, which was one of her favorites. Or maybe Stella
would go home and continue reading the Sue Grafton
novel she had started.

Apartment 1B

She was going to be late again. She just couldn't get herself up and out of the house on time. If Sherry was honest with herself she knew she needed to get to bed earlier. And if she was really honest, she would admit that she didn't like her job and didn't want to be there.

What she wanted to do was write. Most nights she came home from work and after eating a few carrots and pieces of celery, she made herself a mug of tea and sat at her kitchen table with her laptop. The hours passed but Sherry didn't notice. She had been working on her first book for more than a year and saw the story transform from an idea to a novel with a convincing and engaging plot. She was excited about her writing and lived for the nights in her apartment when she could just write.

Some mornings when she was dressing for work she realized she didn't have clean underwear or a blouse to wear. When she checked her laundry basket, overflowing with dirty clothes, she would sigh and pick through the basket looking for something passable that she could iron and wear. This didn't happen just once; after three days in a row of looking for passable clothes in the basket, she finally took the basket downstairs to the laundry room and did a machine of laundry.

Usually she would write herself a note and tape it on her door so that when she got home, before she put the key in the lock, she would read the note that said to bring her laundry downstairs. She would rip the

note off the door, carry it into the apartment and right
to the laundry basket. Then she would turn around
and walk down the two flights to the laundry room.
Of course once it was washed she had to remember to
put her laundry in the dryer and then pick it back up
so she would write two more notes that she kept next
to her laptop. She was about ready to go to bed at
2:15am when she remembered that her laundry was in
the dryer and although she didn't really want to go
downstairs at that time she knew she had to and then
spread her clothes around her living room to be sure
everything was dry before folding and putting it away
the next day.

Housework was not in her plans. She mostly ate off
of paper plates so she never had dirty dishes in the
sink. She bought a turkey breast at the supermarket, a
loaf of wheat bread, and low-fat mayonnaise to make
sandwiches. With that and a bag of apples she was set
for lunches. No dishes, no clean up. Dinner was a
little trickier and sometimes she had a pot to wash
when she opened a can of soup. She knew she
probably wasn't getting the nutrition she needed but
she really wasn't that hungry. Every Sunday she boiled
a half dozen eggs and she would grab one for
breakfast, sometimes dinner, or a late night snack.

Everything she did was to allow her more time to
write. There was nothing else more important to her
than writing. Sleep was a necessity only so that she
could go to work. Working was to buy the minimal
food she needed to survive and to pay for her

apartment so that she had a place to write. That was her focus, her goal, her obsession.

In the shower she worked out a plot she was stuck on. She wrote her ideas on the tile in the shower with a washable crayon she kept in there for that purpose. She dried off and restrained herself from copying her shower wall notes to her laptop. She knew she would never get out of the apartment if she turned on her laptop.

She dressed with clean underwear and a wrinkle-free top and jeans, slathered mayonnaise and sliced turkey on wheat bread, slipped the sandwich into a plastic baggie and put it with an apple into a soft-sided plastic cooler. After smearing a little color on her lips she left for work. Late again. But she smiled as she locked her door and ran down the stairs to the bus stop. On the bus she took out her notebook and continued her thoughts from the bathroom wall. The plot thickened.

Apartment 3B

Beth and Tom lay wrapped in each other's arms when the alarm buzzed. Tom lifted his head and without disturbing Beth, tapped the clock on top. Nine more minutes. He snuggled back into Beth's arms and kissed her neck ever so gently. Then her cheek, her ear, her shoulder. His arousal was instantaneous. Beth smiled, gazing at Tom with half-closed eyes. That was all the encouragement he needed. His mouth covered hers and they embraced deeply.

"Ew, morning breath!" Beth giggled and jumped out of bed. Tom tried to grab her but since she was naked, there was nothing to hold onto. He pounded his fist in the bed and fell onto his back.

"Oh, babe, let's skip work today, whadaya say?"

"I can't. I have a meeting."

"You always have a meeting."

"Yes, I do, often. But so do you." They both worked in the city, 'young professionals' or as they used to call them, 'yuppies', and were both climbing the ladder in their respective businesses; Beth as a marketing manager and Tom as a technology consultant.

"Yeah, yeah. I know. But how about we skip out early, come back here, and make love all night. Please say yes."

Beth came back into the room, teeth brushed and smiling. She loved teasing her new husband. It didn't take much to get him aroused. She knew she had him wrapped he was so crazy in love with her.

"I hate it when you beg." She jumped on the bed, rubbing her breasts all over him, sliding down his stomach kissing as she went, stopping right before she got to his penis. She jumped off the bed and ran to the bathroom where Tom heard the shower running.

"What? Are you kidding me? How can you do this to me? You are plain evil, woman!"

"Ha, ha! Something for you to think about while you are at work today," she yelled from the bathroom and then stepped into the shower, lathering herself quickly. She heard the bathroom door open and close and Tom stepped into the shower behind her.

"There is no escaping now, my love. I will have my way with you."

Beth laughed and turned to Tom, kissing him on the lips. He ran his hands over her soapy breasts and around to her back and with a firm but gentle hold of her buttocks, pulled her to him. He lifted her up and she wrapped her legs around him as he settled her onto him, leaning her against the shower wall. The warm water ran over them, rinsing the soap off her body and down her legs. He kissed her breasts lingering at the nipples. They came together, kissing, touching, loving. They kissed and as they pulled away from each other, Beth grabbed the soap and again, lathered herself.

"Round two?" Tom said hopefully.

"Ha! I was thinking that now you won't hurry home tonight since you've been satisfied."

"I'll never get enough of you."

Beth finished rinsing off and stepped out of the shower. Tom whistled as he soaped up his body.

In the kitchen, Beth had put the coffee on and made them toasted English muffins with peanut butter.

Tom put a couple of roast beef sandwiches together, wrapped them in foil, and put them in lunch bags with an orange. They ate their breakfast at the table in the small kitchenette.

"Remember we have a meeting with the contractor tomorrow night. We have to go over the house plans and give him our changes. We are meeting him at his office at 6pm. Can you make it?"

"I'll be there. And tonight?"

Beth took a sip of her coffee, lifted her eyes to Tom and whispered, "Tonight I'm yours."

Apartment 6B

There was a knock at the door. Geoffrey turned in his chair towards the door, wondering if whoever was there would go away. Solicitors often walked through the building, looking for votes, selling subscriptions, and making any number of door-to-door sales pitches to the tenants in the building. Although the entrance door to the apartment building was locked, somehow they always managed to get into the building where they would walk the halls knocking on doors hoping at least one of them would open, allowing them to go through their spiel. A small part of Geoffrey felt bad for not answering his door; he knew that the people knocking were trying to make a living. He thought that they either didn't have an education and so couldn't get anything better, not even a sales job, or they didn't qualify for any of the available jobs out there. Maybe they were even over-qualified but that was the most unlikely case. More likely was that this was a second or even a third job for some of them.

But deep down, it really didn't matter to him because he would never answer his door. He also knew that most of the people who lived in the building were at work, like the young couple in 3B, the cute, single woman in 1B, and the single mom in 5A. He never knew for sure if the bum in 1A was working or not since he seemed unable to hold down a job. And the older woman in 8A, most likely retired, was in and out of the apartment with her busy life. It seems she was involved in lots of different things and probably kept herself busy so she wouldn't have to think about how sad her life was. The only ones for sure who were probably around were the Switzers in 2A, an elderly couple who stayed in nearly as much as Geoffrey himself did. But just about everyone else in the building was at work.

Geoffrey, recruited by the government right out of college, did a lot of computer forensic investigation work. He preferred to think of himself as a spy but he would never tell anyone that, if he ever talked to anyone. Spying on his neighbors was a hobby; spying on other countries was his job.

He lived in the apartment building longer than anyone else who was currently living there. Many of them came and left, except the Switzers who moved in just after he did, when the building was first built 17 years ago. He got first choice for apartments and chose one as inconspicuous as possible, in the middle but close to the stairs. He thought about an end unit but figured those were the first to get broken into. And definitely he was living upstairs; he felt safer up there. It also gave him the opportunity to set up cameras in the hallways so he could watch the comings and goings of all the units. No one lived a very exciting life, from what he could observe, certainly not as fascinating as his life was. If they only knew they would be shocked, he was sure. And he was pretty sure that what he was doing was illegal and he could get into serious trouble. But he was confident they would never find out about the cameras. No one paid any attention to what was in the corners of the hallways. They left their apartments; they came back to their apartments.

The knock again. The solicitors, whoever they were representing, usually knocked only once and hearing no sounds inside would move on to the next apartment. This one was persistent. Geoffrey remained silent and waited.

Silence was his forte. He imagined that the single man who lived below him would guess that the apartment above him was empty. Geoffrey's persona was to remain invisible to the world which allowed him to travel far and wide unseen and unheard. That was how he was able to be so successful and why the government gave him the most challenging projects. He was very good at his job.

A third knock came. Now Geoffrey was curious. He crept stealthily to his front door and up to the peep hole. He was shocked to see the young woman from apartment 1B. Why was she knocking on his door? He really never talked to anyone and didn't think anyone in the building knew anything about him.

He peeked again out the peep hole. She seemed to be holding a dish, a casserole maybe, in her hands.

"Geoffrey, are you there?"

He jumped back from the door, pushing himself against the wall as if she could somehow see him and he was now invisible. Not only was she knocking at his door persistently but she also knew his name. What to do, what to do? He didn't think he could get out of this one. He had to answer.

He coughed and, after stepping away from the wall, walked up to the door as though he was coming in from the other room. Sliding the chain from the door, he opened it and found himself face to face with the cutest girl he had ever seen.

"Ah, yeah, hi." He wasn't sure what to say and just coughed and shuffled his feet, suddenly uncomfortable in his own place, feeling as if it was he who had just knocked on her door and she opened up to find him standing there.

"Hi, Geoffrey? Yeah, um, my name is Sherry and I live down the hall." She pointed in the direction of her apartment.

"Yeah, so, I made this casserole and I wondered if you might like some?" She seemed as uneasy and nervous as he felt.

"Oh, um, OK." He started to take it but she seemed reluctant to let it go.

"So, um, can I come in and I'll put it on your table? And maybe you could put it in something? Do you have a plastic container or something and then I can just take my casserole dish back? Or you could just bring it to me tomorrow? I mean, if you already ate tonight?"

Everything she said ended in a question. Geoffrey realized she was more unsure of herself than he was.

"I don't cook much, I don't have time to cook, I'm really pretty busy, and I write and work so I don't cook much. But I thought if I cooked a big meal I could eat it for several days and I wouldn't have to think about cooking and I would have plenty to eat but then I realized it was too much and I couldn't eat it all before it went bad. Oh, don't worry; I just made it so it's good, I mean not bad, I mean it isn't spoiled or anything. I don't get out much, I just work in the city and come home and write. I can't believe I'm telling you all this, you don't even know me, each other, I mean we don't know each other, do we?"

The more she talked the more Geoffrey liked her and just like that, he fell in love.

Seven Storied Houses

Cold on the Inside

The Samuelson's lawn and gardens were impeccable. Mike, the gardener, got down on his hands and knees to trim the lawn edges with a pair of shears. The Hydrangeas were deadheaded as were the roses and every other flower when its color began to fade. Each and every tree, shrub, and plant was given individual attention above and beyond what was necessary to maintain a flawless appearance.

The extravagant contemporary mansion was maintained by JJ Webber's Home Renovations. JJ made a lot of money off this one client and appreciated the business. Most of the work he did was unnecessarily redundant. But, of course, he never shared these thoughts with his client. A mostly honest man, JJ also knew a good deal when he was presented with one. And without asking, he always went the extra mile for Mr. Samuelson.

Mike spent more time at the Samuelson's home than JJ did and was in a position to see more of what went on in the 'model' home than anyone else. The Samuelson's also employed a cook, Tessa, and a cleaning woman who was only there on Thursdays.

He figured Tessa was too busy cooking to pay attention to the family dynamics. He occasionally spoke to Tessa just to see what he might add to or change about the opinion he had formed regarding the Samuelsons. Tessa usually didn't have much to add or else she wasn't sharing. She might have thought that Mike was being too nosy. But he was pretty good at getting information and was able to phrase a question in such a way as to appear innocent and having only the best interests of the family in mind. Mike was given a bungalow on the property; one that provided him with a full view of the comings and goings at the Samuelson's home.

"I'm worried about Sunny. She came home pretty late the other night and fell when she was walking up the stairs to the front door. Did you happen to see her? Was she hurt? I almost came out of my place to check on her but then she went inside."

Mike knew Sunny was drunk again. At just shy of 21, she spent most of her nights out with a variety of friends who most likely were leading her down a troubled path that involved alcohol and drugs. Mike would shake his head as he watched her stumble into the home of the wealthy Mr. and Mrs. Edmund Samuelson, owners of Samuelson Real Estate, Samuelson Builders, Samuelson Yachts and several other related businesses. Although he inherited the real estate business from his father, Mr. Sam, as Mike and JJ called him, worked long hard hours to build his empire. Mike thought it disgraceful that Sunny had no respect for a man of her father's stature. She was ungrateful and abusive to Mr. Sam and her mother, calling them bastard, bitch, and whatever other crude word fell out of her mouth at 2am. How on earth could a child like that come out of the front door of such a magnificent home? Mike decided that some kids were just bad. He was hoping Tessa would agree with him, to put his mind at ease that he wasn't just being prejudiced against the girl but that she actually was a bad seed.

"I wouldn't know, Mike. I haven't seen Miss Sunny this morning. You have a nice day now."

Mike would not give up that easily and he continued to ask about Sunny whenever he saw Tessa on the patio setting up breakfast plates or getting ready to drive out to the grocery store to buy lobsters, caviar, or filet mignon for the evening's dinner.

"Are they having a big to-do tonight? Sunny gonna be there? I hope she's OK, seems she hasn't been feeling too good lately, you know?"

Tessa would just wave, with a 'shoo, go away' gesture, and drive off without responding to Mike's many questions.

No one could have guessed what was wrong with Sunny. Not Mike, Tessa, JJ, or Molly the cleaning lady. Neither could Mr. or Mrs. Samuelson know for sure what was wrong with Sunny and why she drank so much and seemed so unhappy and determined to self-destruct before she reached her 21st birthday.

~ ~ ~

Sunny lifted her head off the pillow. She smelled
food. Her stomach growled and then she retched and
ran to her bathroom where she lifted the seat in time
to empty the contents of her stomach, what little there
was in there. Mostly liquid of a color similar to urine.
She wondered if this was in fact pee that never made it
to her urethra but instead came up out of her bladder
and into her mouth looking like vomit. Especially
when there was no food mixed into it. And Sunny
was positive there was no food in there.

First she needed to shower and get the stink off her.
She swished Listerine around in her mouth and spit it
into the shower as she stepped in. The warm water
ran down her face, her stomach, her legs as she slowly
turned, feeling cleansed even without soap. Feeling a
little dizzy, Sunny stopped turning and poured the
shampoo into her hand and rubbed it all over her
head. Then she took the loofah and added liquid
soap, lilac scented, her favorite, to the coarse sponge.
She scrubbed her body briskly and forcefully. The
stimulating strokes with the too warm water produced
an all over red glow, the blood vessels close to
bursting through her skin.

Sunny dried and dressed in shorts and a tank top. Her
breasts rubbed against the soft cotton top causing
stimulation in her nipples she seemed only vaguely
aware of. She touched a hint of shadow on her
eyelids, added a brush of mascara to her lashes, and
the slightest blur of gloss to her lips. She pulled her

still damp hair back into a large barrette and walked down the wide staircase to the kitchen.

"Tessa, is there any breakfast left?" Tessa nearly jumped when the girl walked in. She never knew when Sunny would show up to eat so was sure to always have something kept warm should the child decide she needed some sustenance. This morning Tessa had made Eggs Benedict and saved a good serving for Sunny.

"Well, there you are! Yes, I do have a wonderful breakfast for you, if you'll just sit down I'll fix it right up with some fresh fruit and a glass of juice. What kind of juice would you like, Miss?"

"No juice, Tessa, no fruit, just the eggs, please. And coffee. I'm on my way out."

"Well, you know how I feel about that, Miss Sunny. You really need to eat some good food, you need your strength." If Tessa could only show how she really felt, she would take the girl in her arms and shake her. And then she would hug her. She wanted to cry every time she saw Sunny; she seemed to be shriveling up to nothing. She looked the girl over and noticed streaks of what looked like blood on the backs of her legs.

"What have you done to yourself? Come here and let me look at you." She took Sunny by the hand. Sunny pulled away as if something hot had grazed her skin.

"What? What are you doing? I'm fine."

"No, you aren't. You are bleeding. What is that?"

Sunny turned around to look at the backs of her legs. She saw the bright red marks that the loofah had made. They did look like blood streaks but she assured Tessa she was fine.

"I just scrubbed a little too hard, that's all. It's good to stimulate the skin."

"Stimulating the skin is one thing. Giving yourself 3rd degree burns and shredding your skin is something else!" Tessa shook her head as she poured coffee into Sunny's cup.

"Just half a cup, I'm..."

"I know, you're on your way out."

Sunny smiled, finished most of the eggs, swallowed half a cup of coffee, blew Tessa a kiss, and grabbing her purse off the downstairs table, walked out the front door.

"Don't wait up!"

~ ~ ~

Mrs. Samuelson sat on the veranda sipping her coffee and taking an occasional bite of her fruit salad. She looked out into the gardens, watching Mike trim the hedges. From time to time she turned to the door as if expecting someone to come through it to join her. After turning for the fourth time, Tessa came out and seeing Mrs. Samuelson looking toward the door, answered the question there was no need to ask.

"He's left for the day, ma'am." Mrs. Samuelson gave Tessa a quick smile and turned back to watch Mike while picking at her fruit and sipping her coffee.

"We won't be having company tonight Tessa so just a light dinner is fine. I'll be meeting friends for lunch later. Is Sunny…?"

Rarely did Mrs. Samuelson ask about Sunny. Tessa figured her employer either didn't want to know for fear something horrible had happened to her daughter or, more likely, the woman just didn't care. If Tessa could read her mind she was sure Mrs. Samuelson did not like her daughter. Whenever she had this thought she would shake her head; it was just too repellent a thought to have about a woman and her own daughter. Tessa had a boy and a girl, grown up now, but both in college. She was so proud of each of them and loved them more than she could ever say. And, now, just the hesitation in the woman's voice made Tessa frown and answer a little too curtly.

"Sunny is out. She had breakfast and left." She turned her back to Mrs. Samuelson and carried the dishes into the house. Sometimes she just had to get away for fear of saying what was on her mind. And, at the same time, she feared she would lose a job she had worked at for more than ten years and found to be both comfortable and mostly tolerable. There were a lot worse ones out there.

"Thank you, Tessa." The quiet voice followed her into the kitchen like a waft of bad breath out of a diseased mouth.

~ ~ ~

An early riser, Mr. Sam, Jacob, showered quickly and without waking anyone in the house, left for the office. Since he and Barbara were no longer sleeping in the same bed, he would come and go as he pleased, many days without ever having to talk to her. That seemed to please them both. Driving was sometimes more relaxing for him than a good piece of ass. Of course, that had not been true since he found Georgina. A leggy beauty he met at an international boat show in Dubai, she was there with a group of yachters from the Mediterranean. Jacob fell head over heels and contacted her before he left to fly home. He set her up in a luxury condo with the best of everything. That was six years ago and his heart still skipped a beat whenever she looked at him from across a room, a table, the bed. Although, the situation wasn't perfect for Georgina. She often complained about feeling like a kept woman even though Jacob assured her he was in love and had no intention of leaving her. He even set up a trust fund for her to ease her mind and prove that he would never leave her penniless should anything happen between them.

"You may one day decide you love your wife and go back to her." Georgina would reason with Jacob.

"That will never happen since there has never been any love between us so there is nothing to go back to." A ball of pain formed in the pit of Jacob's stomach and whenever he said these words or others to reassure Georgina, the ball would tighten, causing him to flinch and absentmindedly rub his stomach.

Jacob took the elevator to the penthouse. He quietly opened the door, walked into the bedroom where Georgina was still asleep, and taking his clothes off, slipped into bed beside her. She rolled over and with her eyes still closed gently put her arms around his neck, pulling her naked body closer to him.

"Good morning, gorgeous." His heart skipped a beat as he softly kissed her, starting with her lips.

~ ~ ~

Mrs. Samuelson showered and dressed in a flattering but conservative slim-fitting beige skirt and a short-sleeved pink silk top, buttoned to the top. A small, thin woman by nature, Barbara had no incentive to keep herself in shape but unwillingly followed her friends to the Pilates class every Thursday morning. She would go through the motions robotically and was thankful when the class ended. She never showered at the spa, not wanting any of her friends to see the shapeless, anorexic form she had become. They were all so bouncy, full of energy, and still lovely in their 40's. She felt at least ten years older and ready for the nursing home, frail and withered. She wondered why they even wanted to be around her and she decided they needed someone to make them feel even better about themselves by comparison. She was sure she was their pity friend.

She felt just a bit uncomfortable on this too hot day and wondered if she needed a sweater. Since she had no evening plans, she most likely would not be out at dark when there was often a chill in the air. Lunch and the museum with her three closest friends would make a full day. Tonight she would dine alone.

She checked her image in the mirror while she sprayed a touch of White Shoulders behind her ears. Her short gray-streaked hair did nothing to hide the wrinkles in her neck and the deep creases around her eyes and mouth. Her best friend, Sandy, once told her that she should get a facelift 'if only to get the sadness out of your mouth.' She had looked at Sandy in horror, wondering how she could possibly know what she was feeling inside since she was not a person who shared with anyone, not even her best friend. She certainly never thought of herself as an open book but here was Sandy, usually not a very perceptive person, reading the sadness in Barbara's face. She remained speechless at this comment and excused herself to go to the ladies' room feeling tears forming in the corners of her eyes. Fortunately, when she got back to the table the group was onto another subject and Sandy seemed to have forgotten all about it. Perhaps it was just the 2pm Chardonnay talking.

And now, that was all Barbara could see whenever she looked at her face in the mirror. Sadness. Deep down she knew it was true. She had felt sadness for so many years she didn't know there was any other way to feel. But how can you feel anything but sadness when you are married to the wrong man. And what other feeling could she feel when she felt no love for a daughter who was born to her because she had sex one time with a man she did not love. He was drunk, she was drunk, and they were both rebellious, they had sex, she got pregnant, and as parents did back then when their teens got pregnant out of wedlock, she and Jacob were forced to marry. Of course, Jacob's family had money so Barbara and Sunny never wanted for anything.

Barbara remembered a time when she was in love. His name was Jeffrey. Jeffrey Stuart Morgan. They were together all through high school. They talked about marriage - they were both going to the same college; she was majoring in art and he was going to be an engineer. Everything ended that one night. Barbara remembered so little of it now since it was so long ago. But her life went from the best it could possibly be to the worst she could ever imagine. One mistake; that was all it took was one stupid mistake.

She never saw Jeffrey again. She wondered about him over the years, tried to find him online but there was nothing about him anywhere. That made her wonder if he had died. She heard rumors that he joined the army. He could very well be dead. Then she heard he moved to Spain when he got a job out of college. If he was alive, she hoped he was happy. She would want only the best for Jeffrey.

She looked at her reflection once more in the mirror. Sadness was all that she saw.

~ ~ ~

'Be careful what you wish for you just might get it.' Who'd said that? Sunny knew she'd heard it before but couldn't place it.

"Hey, where did this come from? 'Be careful what you wish for you just might get it.' Who said that? Was it a song?" She thought she was speaking to her friend, Diane, but when she looked around she didn't see Diane anywhere.

"Where's Diane? Diane! Anyone know where Diane is?"

The usual crowd that hung out at Billy's Bar and Grill were gathered around the pool table. There were nine of them if you counted Diane who was, at the moment, missing. Gary and Blake were playing pool. The others were talking and drinking. A couple of people ordered snacks. Lots of laughing, lots of flirting, and lots and lots of drinking.

"I think she's in the bathroom." Someone yelled out over the bar's deafening din.

Sunny got up from the seat where she was sitting and promptly sat down again, missing the chair by about a foot.

"Ooops!" Someone stuck out a hand and she grabbed it and pulled herself up.

"Are you OK?" It was a new guy, someone she hadn't seen before.

"Yup, fine. I gotta go." Sunny turned and walked towards the bathroom. She pushed the door open and staggered in.

"Diane, are you in here?"

"Yeah; I'm sick."

"You mean you're drunk. Ha! Let's go back to my house, you can stay over. Tessa will take care of you."

"What time is it?"

"I don't know... late... early... I don't know. Let's get out of here."

"Who's driving?"

"I'll get a taxi."

"OK."

Taxis hung around outside the bar every night. You didn't have to wait long to get a ride. Sunny and Diane walked out of the bar and walked right up to a taxi driver who opened the back door of his cab. They nearly fell into the back seat and Sunny blurted out her address. They giggled the entire ride to Sunny's house, trying to make conversation with the taxi driver who was unaffected by their drunkenness. He answered their silly questions as sincerely and honestly as he could, despite the slurred pronunciations. A seasoned cabbie, he had seen it all and the two young ladies in the back seat were nothing unusual for him. Almost every night he drove from one to four drunken young women to their homes. At least they weren't trying to drive themselves somewhere, which he appreciated since he had a wife and a little one and another on the way to support. Cabbing was his second job and he knew the later it was the bigger the tips. So, even though he was tired, he drank a lot of coffee and tried to make it to 2am. This ride, at 1:22am, would be his last one tonight.

The taxi pulled up to the gates at the Samuelson's house at around 1:50. The taxi driver stared at the gates and thought it was a gated community for many homes and looked for the gatekeeper to open the gates. But there was no gatehouse.

Sunny rolled down the window of the cab.

"Is anyone there? Mike? Open the gate, it's me, Sunny."

"This is just one house?" The taxi driver asked in disbelief. How could such an ordinary drunk young lady live in such a prestigious home?

"Yup, one house; one fucked up house. How about that?" She pulled a $50 bill from her wallet and gave it to the cabbie.

"Keep the change."

The gates opened as she pulled Diane out of the back seat and they staggered up the driveway together. The gates promptly closed behind them. The cabbie sat there watching the two women walk up the driveway, laughing and stumbling. He shook his head and after several minutes, drove away.

Mike walked back to his room after opening the gate for Sunny and her friend.

"Looks like another drunken night. What is that girl thinking?" He watched her from his front window. "Who is that with her?" The two young women stood at the front door ringing the door bell, laughing and yelling, until it was opened by someone. He hoped they didn't wake Mrs. Sam.

"Foolish girl. She's not gonna learn until something happens. Wait and see." Mike closed his blinds and went back to bed.

~ ~ ~

Although Jacob never wanted to leave Georgina, he did love the game of buying and selling and drove to Samuelson Real Estate office close to noon to see what was in the works. His office dealt with many kinds of properties but he only worked with the multi-million dollar homes. He had a client who was looking for a home on the lake and he had two homes in his price range available for showing. The client was due to come in around 1pm and walked in just as Jacob poured himself a coffee. Surprised to see the client so early, he quickly checked his schedule to be sure he hadn't forgotten the time of the appointment.

"Hello, Adam, what brings you in so early?"

"Hey Jacob, I want to take you for a ride to see a house I want. It isn't on the water but Betty and I drove by last weekend and we both love it. I don't think it is on the market but hey, everything's for sale, right?"

"Absolutely, let me get my keys."

"No, I'll drive." And the two men walked out of the office together.

They made small talk while Adam headed onto the highway. Jacob was involved in telling a story about someone who just bought their first yacht so he didn't notice where Adam was going. A good half hour later, Adam came to a stop.

"Well, here it is. I would love to see the inside but I really like the layout, everything about the outside, so I imagine the inside will be just as perfect."

Jacob turned to look at the house where Adam had pulled up. He got out of the vehicle and stood at the gate, looking in at his home as if seeing it for the first time. This house where he spent so little time. Behind its doors lived a woman he did not love and a daughter he lost long ago. A house, not a home, from which he had fled. A life that was not his own but the result of a stupid kid who fucked up so many years ago. It seemed so unfair that he should spend a lifetime in hell for one mistake. But this was his home, his prison. He suddenly realized that Adam was with him and that he was interested in buying his house.

"So, Adam. I think I could maybe get the owner to sell."

"Really? That would be fantastic! How do you know that?"

"Because it's my house. Make me an offer."

~ ~ ~

Breakfast was a little late this morning. Tessa had some shopping to do and couldn't find what she was looking for, a papaya, so she had to drive to a couple of different stores to find a ripe one. Each morning she made a fruit salad and Mrs. Samuelson specifically requested papaya. Tessa forgot it last week and since Mrs. Samuelson mentioned it again, Tessa was not going to make breakfast without it.

She arrived at the Samuelson home at just a little after 7am. The house was quiet. No one was up yet. She looked in the garage and Mrs. Samuelson's car was there; Sunny's was not. She guessed that meant that Sunny took a taxi, which she had done many times before when she'd had too much to drink. At least that was a good decision. Tessa sighed relief at the thought and went about making breakfast.

The fruit salad made, Tessa set about making the eggs, muffins, and turkey bacon for breakfast. Mr. Samuelson's car was not in the garage but that was not unusual. He spent less and less time at the house. Tessa had her suspicions about where he slept most nights but she would never mention this to anyone. She was a good employee and kept her opinions to herself. Only once or twice she commented about Sunny and her drinking. She feared for the girl and had to share her concerns with Mrs. Samuelson. Mrs. Samuelson, as usual, had no comment in return. She only gazed at Tessa with that same blank sad look in her eyes. Tessa quickly turned away wondering if the look was one of disbelief that Tessa should be so bold. She was, after all, just an employee of the household and never felt like more than that. And then one other time she spoke up, concerning Sunny, but she couldn't remember exactly what she said and it was more of an off-hand comment than an actual criticism of how Mr. and Mrs. Samuelson cared for and disciplined their daughter. After that she pretty much gave up knowing her words were falling on deaf ears.

At quarter to eight Mrs. Samuelson came into the kitchen, fully dressed, made up, and coiffed; looking like she had a date. Tessa wondered how the woman managed to get up every day, where she found the strength. With a stick-thin body and looking so emaciated as if she was recently released from a refugee camp, Tessa did her best to fatten her up. A light eater, Mrs. Samuelson was able to subsist on very little and, therefore, never gained an ounce. Her diet consisted mostly of fruits and vegetables which, although good for you, certainly didn't provide all the nutrition a body needed. Tessa would slip in cheese, salmon, or turkey when she thought she might be able to get away with it but she would often find those little tidbits left on the side of the plate when Mrs. Samuelson had finished her meal.

"Good morning, Mrs. I made a large fruit salad for you and Sunny this morning. I also cooked up some turkey bacon and I was about to cook some eggs. How would you like yours cooked, ma'am?"

"No eggs, Tessa. Just fruit salad and coffee, please. I'll dine on the veranda this morning."

"I already have the table set up for you, ma'am. I'll bring your coffee and fruit salad right out to you. Would you like some turkey bacon? And are you sure I can't make you an egg or two? I could make a couple of nice soft poached eggs on a piece of whole wheat toast."

"No eggs, no toast. Just the fruit salad and coffee, Tessa, please."

Tessa knew better than to ask again. She hoped Sunny was in the mood for a good breakfast but she wouldn't hold her breath waiting for that to happen.

~ ~ ~

Sunny opened her eyes and, once again, awoke to a spinning room and a head that felt three times its normal size. Running for the bathroom, she made it just before the fluids came up out of her stomach and into the toilet.

Then she remembered that somewhere in her room was her best friend, Diane. She was sure of it. At least she was with her when they came into the house. She had a vague memory of being helped up the driveway, or she helped Diane, or maybe they helped each other. She splashed cold water on her face. It felt so good. After drying off, she went looking for Diane.

"Diane, are you in here?"

No response. Sunny hoped she'd had the decency to bring her friend into a guest room and that she hadn't just crashed on Sunny's bedroom floor.

Sunny walked down the hallway to the first guest bedroom. It was the farthest from her mother's room. She knocked briefly and then walked in.

"Diane? Are you in here?" Diane lay sprawled out on the bed, her head hanging over the side. A pile of vomit lay on the rug below her. Sunny got a towel out of the linen closet in the guest bathroom and cleaned up as much as she could, tossing the towel into the bathroom behind the door placing the soiled scatter rug on top of it. The cleaning lady was due to come in and she would find it. She was sure no one else would be using this guest bedroom between now and then.

"Diane, why don't you take a shower? You smell like puke." She giggled a little.

"Look who's talking." Diane mumbled from the bed without moving an inch. Her mouth barely opened to get the words out.

Sunny giggled again. "I know, I smell gross. OK, I'm taking a shower. There are towels in the bathroom closet. If you need anything, I'll be out in a sec. Then we can go have a yummy breakfast. How does that sound?"

Diane groaned. "How about some coffee, or Sprite, and aspirin. I definitely need some aspirin. Hey, did I puke in the bed?"

"No, you puked on the rug next to the bed."

"Oh, god, I'm so sorry. That's disgusting."

"No problem, I cleaned it up."

"You did what? Yuk! You didn't!"

"Well, I didn't really; I just got rid of the rug. It's just a scatter rug so I wiped it up with a towel and threw them in the bathroom. Our cleaning lady will take care of it when she comes in."

"What? No, you can't leave that there!"

"No worries, no one else will come in here. Mother will never come in here. She never even comes down to this end of the house. Probably doesn't even know my bedroom is up here."

"Wow, that's cold."

"Yeah, she is. Well, I'm taking my shower. See you in a few. You can wear some of my clothes if you want, just come and check through my closet. After you've showered, of course." Sunny turned to smile at Diane as she closed the bedroom door.

Downstairs, Mrs. Samuelson sat on the veranda sipping her coffee. She enjoyed being alone in the house and loved to look at the flowering shrubs and beautiful gardens all around her. It was such a lovely home. She really was quite comfortable here. She could easily live out her life in this home with Tessa taking care of the cooking and Andrea, or was it Molly, to do the cleaning. It seemed the service changed her cleaning person from one week to the next and she couldn't keep track of who was now cleaning her home. She told them she wanted the same person each time but apparently they couldn't keep their help. She thought about hiring someone full-time but it was more trouble than she wanted to deal with; finding someone trustworthy who would also do a good job was too much work. She was lucky to have Tessa and it took a long time before she found her. The people who did these sorts of jobs typically were not educated, reliable, or dependable. Barbara insisted that anyone who came into her house to care for it should be all of those things and she didn't think she was being unreasonable. She knew the people who wanted to work and make a good wage were out there. But to take her time to weed out the bad from the good would take far too much time so she used the service. They were bonded so if anything was stolen they would replace it.

She was caught up in her frustration over domestic help when she was abruptly interrupted by voices in the kitchen. She sighed knowing that her moments of silence were coming to an end. She tried to recapture the previous moment she was enjoying and looked up at the sky, at the tree tops gently blowing, and at her lovely gardens.

"Mother, I want you to meet Diane." Sunny walked over to her. Barbara, caught off-guard, jumped up from her seat when she heard Sunny speak. Sunny turned to face Diane and put her arm, uncharacteristically, around her mother's shoulder. Her mother visibly stiffened and seemed to hold her breath for the few brief seconds that her daughter touched her.

Diane felt embarrassed for her friend and nodded slightly to Mrs. Samuelson.

"Hi, nice to meet you." Mrs. Samuelson nodded back. Sunny dropped her rejected arm and turned to go back into the kitchen.

"Tessa, what's for breakfast? Diane wants coffee, anything else, Diane? I'm sure there are eggs, bacon, or whatever you want. Oh yeah, and some aspirin."

Diane looked hard at Sunny who seemed overly bubbly, like she was hiding behind humor so as not to show her true feelings. Diane looked at her friend and thought she detected tears in her eyes. She put her arm around Sunny's shoulder but Sunny brushed her off.

"Let me get you some aspirin."

Diane sat down and Tessa set a mug of coffee in front of her. She poured cream into the cup and stirred it slowly. She felt uncomfortable and thought she should just leave. But she also didn't want to leave her friend if she needed her right now.

Tessa sensed Diane's uneasiness. "She'll be fine. Would you like some eggs, dear? I have some scrambled eggs I cooked up already or I can make some poached or I can boil a couple, whatever you like."

"Thanks, Tessa, that sounds wonderful. I do like to eat breakfast and if you have scrambled already made that will be fine. Thank you."

"I'm happy to have someone here who actually likes to eat real food. I love to cook but no one eats much around here. Would you like a piece of ham with that?"

"Sure, thanks. I'm feeling really hungry now."

Sunny walked back in the room and put a bottle of aspirin on the table.

"We should go. We have to get our cars. I'll have Mike drive us or we can just take a taxi. Are you ready?"

"I was going to eat. Tessa just dished up some eggs for me and I'm really hungry."

"I thought you had a headache?"

"I do but having the coffee is making it feel a little better and I think eating some eggs will really help, too."

"Yuck, how can you eat?"

"I have to eat breakfast." Diane realized that Sunny just wanted to get out of the house so she took several good bites of the wonderful breakfast, a few gulps of coffee with a couple of aspirin, and cutting up the slab of ham, stabbed a couple of pieces with egg and chewed quickly, preparing to leave the house with Sunny.

"Oh, go ahead, eat. It will make Tessa happy, right Tessa?"

"It is nice to have someone eat something more than just fruit and drink coffee."

"Thanks, this is great, Tessa. You are an amazing cook."

"Well, thank you dear."

Sunny paced around the kitchen, sipping her coffee. Occasionally she glanced towards the veranda and with squinted eyes and a firm mouth, glared at her mother through the window. Her mother's back was toward the kitchen so she missed the look from Sunny. But Tessa saw it. So did Diane.

~ ~ ~

Jacob sat at his regular table at Café Bistro waiting for Georgina to arrive. He sipped his Glenfiddich, staring out the window at the boats in the harbor. Jacob loved the water, loved his yacht and often imagined himself setting sail with Georgina for the Hawaiian Islands and living there forever.

His regular waiter, Joe, was at his table setting down a Chardonnay at Georgina's seat. Joe turned and watched Georgina as she seemed to glide across the floor, her dark brunette hair flowing around her as if a fan was directed right at her face just to get this effect. Her perfectly shaped breasts moved freely under her sheer floral dress held up only by spaghetti straps and a tightly fitted sash that accentuated her 19 inch waist. Tanned slender legs on 2" matching floral heels carried this vision of pure feminine seductive beauty to Jacob's table. Jacob slowly stood as he took in every inch of her into his vision. Joe, smiling, imagined that every man who watched Georgina walk from her car into the restaurant and towards Jacob's table was fantasizing that she was theirs, that she was walking towards their table, and that they would have her in their bed that night.

Jacob took her hand, kissed it, and leaned in to kiss her on her cheek. He pulled her chair out and, as she sat, breathed deeply the scent of Shalimar that was now Georgina's fragrance. He sat down next to her.

"You look positively gorgeous, Geo. I can't tell you how aroused I am right now. You drive me crazy."

Jacob reached over and took her hand, kissing the palm and sticking one of her fingers into his mouth.

Georgina, a little embarrassed, pulled her finger out of Jacob's mouth, looking around the restaurant at the other customers. The men were all still staring, unable to take their eyes off the vision at Jacob's table, despite the stern looks from their dining companions.

"Not in the restaurant, please Jacob. We will have plenty of time to be together tonight. Can't you wait?"

"No, I can't."

"Well, you must. Now, let's have a nice dinner, OK? Will you be staying tonight or do you have to go home to your family?"

Jacob shook his head. His family. What family? A wife who couldn't stand him, and the feeling was mutual, and a daughter who had no interest in him. Of course that was his fault more than it was hers. His ghost family, invisible to him but still very real. He knew they were there even though he never saw them. His family was Georgina. She was his real family.

Sunny. He hated himself for how he treated Sunny, how he and Barbara both blamed her for their mistake. It wasn't fair to the girl. Jacob had to make it up to her. But how? He was sure she didn't approve of his relationship with Georgina, if she even knew about her. She had to know about her. Sunny was almost 21 and she had to know what was going on.

But he had to make it up to her; he had to somehow, before it was too late. Before he lost her forever. Maybe he should set up a lunch date with her. But, hadn't he done this before? She didn't show up. He had to figure out a way to get to Sunny, to apologize for all those years, so many years, of not being there for her. He had to tell her it wasn't her fault.

"Jacob?" Georgina was waiting for a response.

"Yeah, baby, I'll come back to the condo with you. Of course, that's where I want to be. With you, always." He took her hand and kissed it ever so gently.

Jacob thought about his house and the offer from Adam. He couldn't do it to Sunny; he couldn't sell the house right out from under her. He didn't think about Barbara for a minute. She had been enjoying the sweet life for so long now. But for Sunny, he would keep the house. He wanted to share this news with Georgina, but to her it would only mean that he still had strong connections to his family. He wanted her to understand that it was only Sunny he felt anything for and kept his house, even though he was rarely ever there, only because of Sunny. He would figure something out, some way to get her away from drinking so much. Mike let him know what was going on at the house. Mike saw Sunny coming home drunk every night. Jacob had to help her before it was too late. He had to be there for her.

"Things are going to change, baby, I promise you."

"I believe you, Jacob. Now let's get some food!"

Jacob smiled, kissed her hand again, and opened his menu.

~ ~ ~

Sunny and Diane took a taxi back to the night club where they were the night before to get their cars.

"So, what do you want to do today? Beach?" Diane loved the beach and that was usually her first suggestion.

"Oh, I don't know. I might go shopping. How about going to Lulu Bahama's and having a Mimosa?"

"Yuck, are you kidding? I can't even think about alcohol right now." Diane was pretty sure Sunny was not kidding. She seemed so distracted. Diane wished she could get Sunny out of this funk she was in, but she was pretty sure she couldn't. There were things beyond her control.

"Well, aren't you boring all of a sudden. Maybe I'll just go alone."

Diane didn't want to leave her friend alone right now. She knew Sunny was not in a good place and decided she needed to stay close to her.

"I like the shopping suggestion. Why don't we do that. Maybe we can go to Lulu's later?"

"OK, but we have two cars."

"Follow me home and you can drive." Diane decided that since Sunny had a sporty Mercedes that was a lot more fun to drive around in than her practical Honda Accord that Sunny wouldn't risk driving drunk. Diane knew Sunny wouldn't want anything to happen to her little sports car. The plan was spontaneous but Diane hoped it was solid and that she could keep Sunny safe.

Sunny bought a couple of new outfits and even insisted on buying a couple of pairs of shorts for Diane. They had a quick lunch at TGI Fridays, where Sunny had just one beer, and then drove to the beach. They found their usual crowd of friends there and hung out until someone mentioned going to LuLu's.

"I'm there, coming with me Diane?" Diane was talking to Dan, a guy she really liked. She seemed like she didn't want to go or else she wanted to go with Dan. She waved at Sunny to go on without her.

"Fine, fuck you bitch." Sunny sped off in her convertible and arrived at Lulu's before everyone else. She was on her second dry martini by the time the others arrived. She was in the mood to dance and grabbed Dan when he walked in with Diane.

"Come on, big guy. How about a dance?" She rubbed herself up and down his leg and kissed him on the neck when she came up his leg.

"Sunny, stop!" Diane was getting angry.

"What? Oh, are you guys a couple now?" Dan didn't know what to do and started backing away. Diane grabbed Dan by the arm and they walked away, leaving Sunny alone on the dance floor.

"Yeah, well, fuck you, Diane! Who needs ya?" She turned away, grabbed her purse from the table where she had been sitting, and left.

~ ~ ~

Jacob was determined to make amends with Sunny. After another fabulous night of lovemaking with Georgina, he left her with the promise to be back later that day. She knew he loved her and would never go back to his wife. And she agreed that he needed to take care of Sunny. He needed to do what he could to have some kind of a relationship with her. It was time. It was past time. Sunny needed him. It was time for him to step up and be a dad for once. She needed his help. Sunny was never going to get it from her mother.

On the way over to his house he stopped at the florist to pick up a bouquet of tulips for Sunny. He remembered that they were her favorite flowers when she was a little girl.

"They look like bonnets." Sunny had said. Jacob smiled when he remembered the first time he brought them home for her when she was just six years old. He wasn't sure what her favorite color was so he got her one of each color they had at the florist. She ran into the kitchen and got a vase from under the kitchen counter, filled it with water, and one by one put the tulips into the vase. She took such care and tenderness with each tulip like each one was an individual person and deserved special attention.

"Here daddy, put them on the kitchen table, please."

"But daddy bought them for you, princess. Don't you want me to put them in your bedroom?"

"No, daddy, I want everyone to see them. Something so beautiful should be enjoyed by everyone."

Even now he was amazed at her wisdom and generosity at such a young age. His eyes began to blur as he drove up to the gate of his house. The gate, usually closed, was open and Jacob drove right in. There were three police cars in front of the house and Jacob jumped out of his car and ran in the front door.

"What the fuck's going on?" Barbara stood facing him, the three cops standing in front of her. They all turned when Jacob came in the door.

"Mr. Samuelson, I'm so sorry sir. There's been an accident."

"What accident? What do you mean an accident?" He looked at Barbara who was staring at the floor, concentrating all her attention on the shattered glass that lay there. She broke her concentration just long enough to look at Jacob. Jacob looked at her and then at the cops and then back to Barbara.

"What accident?"

"Sunny." Barbara stared at Jacob. Jacob stared at Barbara. Her eyes were dry, not a single tear was shed. Jacob slowly walked upstairs, packed a suitcase with some clothes, and walked out of his house for the last time.

Seven Storied Houses

Finding My Abled-ness

The sun is hot on my face, my arms below my pastel plaid short-sleeved shirt, and my legs below my chino shorts. If I was sitting in a chair, my knees would be bent and from the knees down my legs wouldn't be quite so hot. But my mom insists on sitting me in the chaise lounge with my legs straight out like a Ken doll. If I complain she will tell me, once again, that I need Vitamin D.

"If you don't have Vitamin D you'll die. This is the best way to get it, from the sun. Your body, every part that is exposed, will just soak it up. You'll thank me later."

We both know this is unlikely to happen. I rarely complain about anything my mom does and when I do complain, it sounds more like a howl than any intelligible words. In my mind, I am talking in complete sentences but something happens between my brain and my mouth. The two are obviously sworn enemies and most likely wonder how they ended up in the same body. Tough luck for me.

My mom comes out through the screen door carrying a glass of lemonade with ice and a straw.

"Here you go, sweetie. I know it's hot out here but you can sit a bit longer and then I'll bring you in. I just hate seeing you sitting in front of that TV day in and day out. You need to get some fresh air. And God knows, you can't go out in the winter, it is just too damn cold and it would take me forever to get enough clothes on you to send you outdoors. And then what would you do? You would just sit in the snow and your hands and toes would freeze because God knows you can't move and I would have to call your Uncle Joey to take you to the hospital and they would probably have to remove some of those fingers and toes that turned black from the frostbite. And it would be a mess. So, instead, I put you out here in the sun and let your body suck up that Vitamin D. Isn't that nice?"

I suck on the straw draining the glass in about the same time it takes her to recite her diatribe on the evils of winter in New England for her differently-abled son. This is her term for me. She thinks that the many ways my disability has been labeled are so inaccurate and don't at all describe what my life is like. But she saw the term 'differently-abled' in a thesaurus and thought this was the best way to describe her son to people who were curious and nosey enough to ask. Now, what she was doing looking in a thesaurus is something you would have to ask her. But suffice to say, this is who I am to my mom.

I kind of like it, too, because first of all, it says I'm different. As much as we all want to be the same, we also want to be different, or rather, special. And of course, 'abled' means I have abilities; I am not just a vegetable sitting here, unable to speak or communicate in any way. I have talents of some kind or other. What they are I have yet to discover. But I know that somewhere deep inside me I am 'abled' in some way. I believe I do have abilities.

The lemonade is wearing off and now I feel sweat running down from the top of my head. It tickles behind my ears and I smile. Or at least my version of a smile. I've been told I look like I'm feeling pain and my mom will ask me if I'm OK. I think she believes that, like a baby, I'm experiencing gas bubbles. Mostly I'm smiling about something funny she said, or that someone on TV said. Although TV is rarely very funny, it is mostly just stupid. I don't think I have any expression for that but if I did it would look like a wise-ass kid with a smirk. I'm pretty sure I can't do that. Maybe that will be one of my abilities. Maybe I'll copy expressions people make and people could guess what I'm expressing. I don't know but I hope my abilities are a little more cerebral than that.

I feel the sweat under my arms. I'm getting uncomfortable now. My mom is pretty good at determining my level of comfort from one experience to the next. It is like we are connected in more ways than just through my birth. As if a part of her is in me and a part of me is in her. It is pretty cool most of the time. Sometimes she is a little too close for comfort.

Sometimes I want to feel more independent. Although I know that is unlikely to ever happen, not in this lifetime anyway. Maybe if I get the chance to come back in another lifetime. And if I do, it better be as a Brad Pitt clone or someone really handsome and sexy like that. Or hey, maybe even a woman, that would be OK, as long as it's not a clone of me.

I figure I must have been a really bad dude in a previous life and this is my punishment. My mom thinks I am a blessing. Of course, she isn't in my body and doesn't have to live this life. But on some level, I guess she really is living this life with me since she can't do much because she has to take care of me all day long. She can go out and food shop or visit Uncle Joey and Aunt Sally for a couple of hours at a time. And she has a friend, Sophie, who stops by and brings cinnamon Bundt cakes and chocolate chip cookies or sometimes mom visits her. But I can't really do anything so I wonder if this, my life, is a punishment. 'If you aren't part of the solution you are part of the problem.' Who said that? I'm not coming up with any solutions so I must be part of the problem. Just taking up space. Not serving any purpose. Purpose.

So since this life is a punishment we'll just get this out of the way for my sins in past lives and my next life will be something wonderful, I'm sure. Sometimes I think about that and want to end it all and get on with the next life. But how would I do it? I can't pick up a gun to try to blow my brains out or even pick up a bottle of pills so that I may end this life. I'm doomed to live this life out for however long it takes.

I don't know how much longer I can sit here. I am getting really uncomfortable now. It feels as if someone just turned up the heat in the sauna another 50 degrees. Maybe I'm having a hot flash. But I think those are reserved for women. Although sometimes I feel a flash of heat come over me and I can't explain where it is coming from. If I was in the tub, I could see how the heat would get to me after sitting there awhile. But it will happen when I'm just sitting on the sofa or about to go to sleep in my bed. For no reason. Maybe it has something to do with my different-abled-ness. Since I'm not sure what my problem is, really, I just always file everything under that same category. If something doesn't work for me the way I observe how it works for other people, I decide that is yet another symptom of my different-abled-ness. For example, I can't pick up silverware to eat my own food, I can't walk, I can't talk, I can't climb into a bathtub by myself, I can't dress myself, I can't pick up stuff, I can't skip or run or ride a bicycle. I do like to watch the kids in the neighborhood doing these things, though, especially riding a bike. That looks like so much fun.

There are a few things I can do that really help my mom. I didn't know how to communicate to her that I needed to use the toilet. For too many years I sat in my own poo. Talk about uncomfortable! I was upset to see what my mom had to do to clean up after me. Not to mention it was humiliating to me. So, I came up with something I could do; I worked at it for the longest time, too. I roll my eyes around 3 times. Of course, I had to train my mom to understand what

exactly I was doing. The first time I did this she
thought I was having a seizure and rushed me to the
hospital. I don't think the doctor and nurses who
attended to me appreciated the accident that was
waiting for them in my pants. It didn't take my mom
too long after that to figure it out. The next time I
rolled my eyes 3 times she brought me a glass of water.
Too late. I think it was by the third time that she got
it. She had put me to bed, I guess thinking my eye-
rolls indicated I was tired. So, my underwear and my
sheets needed cleaning that time.

"So, when you roll your eyes 3 times, you need to go
poo? Is that right, honey?"

I smiled.

"You got gas, sweetie?"

As if on cue, mom comes out to roll me back in.
Fortunately she is a strong woman. She always tells
me I'm light as a feather.

"I need to fatten you up, feed you more of Sophie's
cake. You feel like you weigh nothing at all. It's so
surprising, it is, since I always thought love and
sweetness were heavy on the heart. And since I know
those are the main ingredients in you, my darlin', you
should weigh 300 pounds. You are just full up of love
and sweetness."

She wheels me in and sets up my chair in front of the
TV.

"Do you want to sit in your chair?"

I looked up at my mom and then down, which is another way I help my mom know what I want. That means, "Yes."

"OK, I'm gonna go fix us some supper. One of your favorites tonight, fried chicken with mashed potatoes and green beans. Yum!"

I smile and then not smile three times to let mom know when I really like something. And yes, I do this for fried chicken, mashed potatoes, and green beans. Well, maybe not so much the green beans, but it is all good. And she is a great cook. It really is surprising I'm not heavier, although I'm not quite a feather-weight as mom says I am. She's just being nice.

The History Channel is on. Mom knows I like this channel and unless I indicate otherwise (I move my eyes from right to left which is basically the same thing as shaking my head 'no') she usually puts this channel on. I always learn something on the History channel. I've been hoping that history, in whatever form they show it, will help me find purpose, meaning, and my abled-ness in this life. Actually, that is the main reason I watch any TV at all. Sometimes, on the PBS channels, they show psychologists or experts trained in helping people find themselves and live better lives. I watch PBS a lot, too. Nothing has spoken to me yet.

An "Ancient Aliens" show is on. I like this show. I can watch them all day. At first she would judge a particular show I was watching, thinking it wasn't appropriate for me to see.

"This is crap, sweetie, you don't want to watch this. There has to be something better on. Let's find you a nice sit-com. They are usually funny and I think you'll like that better."

I hate sit-coms. Most of them are not funny at all, except maybe "The Big Bang Theory." That is really funny. I can binge-watch that show all day, too. So, teaching my mom the shows I like has been really difficult, she has to pay really close attention to my face, mostly my eye movements but also my smiles. So now when she puts a channel on, if it is something I haven't watched before, she will wait and watch my face after I've watched an episode or two. If I keep my eyes down and don't smile, she knows I don't like it. The three smiles, not smiles means it is a hit. She's learning. She has actually picked up really fast on my cues considering I only have my eyes and smiles to convey messages to her.

I thought Ancient Aliens, like the PBS shows that feature psychologists, might show me something about our history that could direct me to the meaning of life when you don't have a real life on this planet. Although each episode is almost more interesting than the last one, I haven't found anything that would help me find my abled-ness. If anything, I feel even more insignificant. But I don't think that is just me. I think that most people who watch the show or other similar shows that talk about the age of our planet and the people who have been here before us feel equally insignificant. It makes you realize how huge the world is and we're each like a grain of sand in an hourglass.

Of course, that helps since I already feel insignificant. Misery loves company, as they say. But there are many, many people who contribute so much to society. Those are the people I want to be like. Those are the people I admire. They are part of the solution. They have found their abled-ness and are making a difference in life. For everyone. They aren't just living a self-centered existence, doing what they please at the expense of the planet and every living being on it. And I'm not talking about just the people on the planet. I'm talking about the elephants, the whales, the hummingbirds, the ants and every other creature, great and small. Every one of them counts and deserves to have a nice home, good health, and plenty of clean air and water. If I could find something, somehow, that I could do to make a big difference in so many lives, that would truly be finding my abled-ness.

My mom walks into the room and straight over to me. She plants a kiss on the top of my head.

"Dinner is ready, my love. Do you want to stay in here and I'll feed you so you can continue to watch your program?"

I indicate that we can go into the kitchen by signaling 'no.' She understands that when I indicate no, she can usually go with the other option. And most times there is only one other option. She wheels me into the kitchen and right up to the table. Even though I can't feed myself, she always makes sure that it appears as though I can. There is a plate in front of me with a fried chicken breast, about a dozen string beans, and the size of a fist of mashed potatoes, all of which is more than enough for me. I will probably only eat about half of everything that is on my plate. I do want to keep my weight down because I know that as mom gets older it will be harder for her to lift me up and into my chair, my bed, and the tub.

Mom wraps a dishtowel around my shirt collar, just in case there is 'droppage.' Unfortunately there usually is. The food mostly stays in my mouth but sometimes I can't swallow and get it down before another piece is headed my way. It isn't mom's fault, she thinks I'm done and can't tell there is more in there that I just haven't gotten to chew up yet.

"Oh darlin', I'm so sorry, are you OK? Here, have a sip of water and rinse it all down. Lift your eyes up and down once when you are ready for more."

She leans over and gives me a kiss on my cheek. I smell lemons. I love smells, I don't know the names of most of them, but mom and I figured out that lemons make me smile. I think she puts some kind of splash on, eau de lemon, or something like that. She said it makes her feel fresh and clean. I think she started wearing it more often when she knew I liked it.

I finish my meal without too much trouble. Mom has patience beyond belief and sticks with it no matter how long it takes. I am so grateful for everything she does and has done over the years. If I had one wish it would be to have just a few minutes of time to be able to tell mom how much I love her and what she has done, what she has sacrificed, to care for me. I don't think this is for everyone. I think a lot of people would give up, would put their child in some kind of home. They just would not have the patience, the time, the love to care for a child who needed the level of care that I need.

Mom wipes my mouth with a napkin and takes the dishtowel off, depositing the crumbs into the trash. She wheels me back into the living room and finds the channel that has 'The Big Bang Theory' on it. I've seen many of the episodes at least twice but they are still funny. And sometimes there is a joke or something funny that I missed the first couple of times I saw it.

Two or three hours go by and I yawn. Mom is up and beside me in a snap.

"Ready to go to bed, hon?"

I look up and then down. We head for the bathroom where I have my final visit to the toilet. I haven't had many accidents over the years and I feel so terrible when I do. But mom and I worked it out and I don't get any liquids after 7pm. Mom brushes my teeth and after giving me water through a straw, holds an empty Cool Whip bowl under my chin so I can spit.

"Good job, sweetie! Teeth feel all nice and clean now, don't they. And now we're off to bed. I think I'll stay

up for a while and catch the news. I could read to you
for a bit if you'd like."

I move my eyes left to right.

"OK, you get some sleep. I would say beauty sleep
but it seems you've already had plenty of that, my
beautiful boy!"

I smile.

Mom lifts me into bed, kisses my forehead, and
touches my face with her hand, pushing my hair back
as if it is hanging in my eyes. She sits on the edge of
my bed as she does this. She is humming and kisses
my forehead, each cheek, and the tip of my nose.

"I love you, my darlin'."

I smile, not smile three times.

Seven Storied Houses

A Funeral in the Family

'Bump, bump, bump, I'm hooked on believing, I'm high with this feeling, that you're in love with me'. Or is it 'that I'm in love with you'? Neither seemed right, except the bump, bump, bump part. That was the blood vessel deep within her skull, a nagging reminder that she drank more than she could handle. Again.

"You have to stop doing this. Yes, I know, except I don't know how. One of the many life skills I was never taught since my parents were clueless about so many things. What did they teach me again? Oh yea, how to feel like shit about myself all the time. How to drink my sorrows away – except they forgot to tell me that they come back again when you are sober. What else? There are just so many things. How to live your life at the bottom, forever in debt, unloved, stressed out, anxious about everything from paying my rent, to getting a better job, to living a clean, successful life. I believe many of those are in the top ten list for how not to be a success in life without really trying."

And this was even worse than everything else, the pity party. And the puking. Sam jumped out of bed and ran to the bathroom, her head pounding louder than ever, and lifted the toilet cover just in time before the entire contents of her stomach heaved out onto the floor. She stood over the bowl, the smell of urine wafting up, causing her to heave again, stronger and more painful than the first time, tears streaming down her face. Not a bowl hugger, standing over the bowl was as close as she wanted to get to the place where she emptied her bowels. That always did the trick when she was trying to puke. She just had to lift the cover and the puke would come up, without any coaxing at all. She never understood when people talked about hugging the bowl, though. Seriously, getting down there with your face hanging over the ceramic rim? She just couldn't imagine getting that close. She would have to scrub the entire thing until it shined, which would never happen because when you have to puke, you puke, there is no pause button.

But puking did always make her feel better. Stomach empty, she still wasn't ready to put food into it. She did have to get up and get ready for the funeral. The funeral. She said it so easily, so naturally in her mind, like potatoes or Kleenex. Yes, I'll have some more potatoes, thank you. Funeral usually brings up sadness and pain in most people. She felt nothing. It was just something she wanted to get over with so she could get on with her miserable life. Meeting up with the family was never something she looked forward to, it was just another thing to get through until the next family obligation came along.

Back in bed, Sam knew she had to pull herself together and get ready. Lightheadedness washed over her like a cold shower, shocking her eyes open as she focused on her surroundings. Last night's clothes were strewn around the room like they would be when she brought someone home who was as much in heat as she was and the clothes were a barrier to a brief moment of animal lust. She had no memory of removing her own clothes but there was no sign of the lucky guy so she figured her memory, at least when she staggered in last night, was not functioning. This always scared her if she let herself think about it. OK, so she didn't remember an action as simple as removing her clothes and getting into bed, but she did drive home. She definitely did not remember the drive home but here she was, safe and sound, in her own bed. Someone was looking out for her. But who, and why? It wasn't like she was living such a compassionate life, saving the planet. No one would miss her if she died, no one. What was there to save anyway? Hers was just another wasted life in a pond full of scum.

And the pity party goes on. Another wave of nausea ran over her but this time the feeling was for food, not the need to puke. This was an improvement. Sam headed to the bathroom and a shower first. That always made her feel better, too, whether or not she was hung over. The water ran down her face as she slowly turned, wetting her head, letting the water completely cover her. She closed her eyes, but tipped to the right as she continued to turn in the tub. She quickly opened her eyes as nausea flowed over her again and she squatted down in the tub to suppress the sick feeling. Not a good idea to turn with her eyes closed.

After drying off and wrapping her hair in a towel, she headed to her kitchen to look for food. Did she shop? She couldn't remember. Scrambled eggs, that sounds great. Oh please, let there be eggs. Now she was feeling really hungry. She opened the refrigerator door- yes, she shopped, yes, there were eggs. She whipped up the eggs, toasted a whole wheat English muffin, and made a mug of Pips tea. She flipped through her International Artist magazine while slowly eating breakfast, carefully chewing each piece envisioning every nutrient attaching itself to the part of her body that needed it most. She was beginning to feel more life-like, so clean, like a newborn. Good health surged through her veins. She could almost understand why some women became bulimic- puking was rejuvenating in a way. You get rid of the toxins and then you can start fresh and put good food into your body.

She looked up at the clock, 11:25. What time is the funeral? 1pm, right? She wrote it down somewhere. So, first the wake and then the funeral immediately following. They seemed to be doing that these days instead of dragging out the wake for a couple of days and then another separate day for the funeral. It has to be stressful for the family when they have to greet people again and again at the wake, receiving their condolences for the deceased, standing there hour after hour, appearing strong. And then after the funeral they have to feed all these people. What is that all about! Sam thought at that point they should all just go home and leave the poor family to their mourning. At most wakes, anyway. Sam knew that her mom would perform exceptionally well in that role, as would Jack and Paula. The perfect family, always. Until Sam shows up. Funny. At least that is how she sees herself and she is pretty sure that Jack and Paula see her that way, too. Maybe even her mom, to a certain extent. Sam is, after all, the 'messed up' one, as her mom so fondly referred to her one time.

Since she only lived about ½ hour from the church, she knew she had plenty of time to get there. She quickly put on her only black dress, a straight shift with a slit up the back, sleeveless with a scoop neck. This has been her all-occasion dress for many events. She doesn't remember what she paid for it but whatever the cost, she certainly got her money's worth out of it. Sam didn't like spending a lot of time with makeup and had a routine down that took her about 5 minutes for everything. Drying and styling her hair took the longest but she decided to pull back her auburn hair into a ponytail. She was ready to go with minutes to spare.

As she drove off in her used Toyota Camry, she knew she should have searched for the correct time of the funeral.

"Damn, I hope I guessed right." She was pretty sure she was right, it sounded right. It was the first time that came to her so it had to be right. Sam turned the radio on to help drown out the guilt voice in her head. Unfortunately the voice in her head had a big mouth and she thought about turning around and driving home to find out the exact time but decided instead, since she was about half way there, to just continue toward the funeral home.

She arrived at Blake's funeral home at almost exactly 1pm. She thought everyone, meaning her immediate family, would be surprised to see her arriving on time for a change. She parked in the nearly full parking lot and walked in the front door. Sawyer party to the left, Gilden party to the right. Party, yeah this is a party, where's the music, the noise-makers, and most importantly, where's the wine? Sam walked into the left entrance and caught Paula's eye. Paula, standing next to Jack who was standing next to her mom, waved her over.

"Where have you been? Why do you always have to be late?"

"Late, what do you mean late, how am I late?" Then for the first time Sam noticed that the room was already full of people, several standing in line waiting to share their condolences with Sam's mother.

"This started at 12:00 and we've all been here since 11:30."

What the fuck! How could she be so wrong about the time. Sam couldn't believe it. Her mom was right, she really was the messed up one. Or maybe it was a case of self-fulfilling prophecy. Because her mom said she was messed up, she had to prove that her mom was right. She knew she should have gone home to check the time, although that would have made her even later so no, coming here when she did and being just an hour late was the right thing to do.

Jack turned and glared at Sam. She knew that look. *"You are so disappointing not only to me but to mom as well, just when she needed all of us so much. Good thing I am here for her."* Sam flashed a toothy smile at him and looked around the room. No one she wanted to talk to so she continued to stand next to Paula. She supposed it was where she should be anyway since it was, after all, her dad who was lying in the box. She glanced at the box. She could barely see his profile as he lay in the box wearing his Sunday best dark blue suit. She seemed to remember seeing him wear the suit only about 4 times in her life. To weddings, mostly. She could see his face, still bloated, still blushed from the last breath he took after he finished the last bottle of booze he would ever drink. Of course, the blush on his cheeks could also be from some of the pancake makeup they smear on you to make you look like you're still alive even though all your fluids have been removed from your body. A cartoon pops into her head of her dad lying on the coroner's table, the fluids draining from his body while his body deflates like a blow up doll losing its air. All that is left is a rubbery suit of skin. She smiles in spite of herself and looks away to distract her thoughts. Again, Jack is glaring. It's the same look so she assumes he's thinking the same thing as before; Poor mom, Sam is such a disappointment. If he had a child like her... well, obviously he wouldn't. Sam thought about Jack having a daughter or even worse, a son, like her. Again, she smiled. She looked up to see Aunt Clare, the matriarch of the family now that all the other relatives were dead, looking at her with the oddest look on her face. Sam waved at Aunt Clare.

"Hi, Aunt Clare, how are you?" Sam thought it best to keep her distance. Aunt Clare was either losing her hearing or was suffering from some form of dementia because any conversation with her was so scattered that Sam had a hard time following the story line, even when Sam was completely sober. Aunt Clare continued to glare at her with an almost angry look on her face. Oh no, Sam thought, she must have talked to Jack.

"Oh, hello dear, I didn't see you there. How are you doing?" Didn't see me, Sam wondered, she was staring right at me. Maybe she was at the age where you start seeing leprechauns, trolls, and other such bizarre creatures instead of people. Sam thought about how old she was and guessed she might be around 90 now. Pretty old. If Sam ever made it to 90, which she strongly doubted she would, she wanted to die in her sleep and not have to suffer with pain, hooked up to a machine, pumping drugs into her body to keep her breathing and her heart beating and out of pain. Of course this thinking followed with the next logical thought, I must make out a will. And that was followed with, why? What on earth do I have to leave anyone?

"I'm fine, Aunt Clare, just fine. Nice to see you." She looked away hoping that would end any further dialogue. It did. When she looked back at Aunt Clare, Cousin Kathy with her husband Mike, and two teenagers, Randy and Sherry whose emotionless faces reflected exactly how Sam felt, were greeting Aunt Clare, hugs all around, except for the teens who couldn't see Aunt Clare beyond their iPhones.

Sam was ready to go home but knew this was going to take several more hours. And then, of course, the dinner back at mom's house after the funeral. And then she was on her own. She should call Stacy, see if she was up for a night on the town. It was Saturday so she didn't have to get up early in the morning. Although she should paint, too. Unless her plan was to be a waitress her entire life.

Painting was the one bright light in Sam's life. When she put out fresh oils, the rich smell wafting up to her nose, breathing in the colors, some stronger than others, it just made her want to sing. She dipped the brush into the thick blob of color and touched the naked canvas, smearing it across the white surface. She usually didn't have a plan when she started to paint, it all just came to her as she went along and she was pretty happy with the results thus far. She figured her muse was taking over and she gave in to its desires. Sam also enjoyed a couple of one-person shows where she sold several large pieces – the money kept her going for a while, paying her rent, groceries, utilities, and other necessary bills, but then she would nose-dive and come up gasping for air, head over the bowl again.

She was never quite sure how this happened but she thought it had something to do with having to prove herself again and again. Not just to herself but to her perfect, judging, controlling family. A part of her felt she was following in her drunken father's footsteps, too. An unhappy postal worker, her dad had spent most nights in the barroom, drinking away whatever intelligent thoughts might have spawned other creative thoughts to do something more with his life, to spend more quality time with his family, to make something of himself before his life was over. Obviously, those thoughts never came to fruition. He chose D, none of the above. Sam figured at some time he must have had goals, hopes, and dreams but she never saw any evidence of them. She got the worst of Dad. Who knows when you lose your will to be all that you can be. She's guessing it's somewhere around her age, early thirties.

"I have to go to the bathroom", Sam whispered to Paula. "I'll be right back."

"OK, but don't be too long." There it was, the big bossy sister attitude. Sam decided that comment didn't need to be acknowledged and she just walked away.

She passed one of the funeral home employees and grabbed him by the arm, "Hey, can you tell me where the bathrooms are?"

"Yes, ma'am, go down this hall and down the stairs. First door on your right."

Ma'am, she hated that.

"Really, downstairs? What if I was in a wheelchair?"

"We have a special handicap bathroom upstairs."

"And I can't use that one?"

"Well, it is special for people in wheelchairs. So, yes, you have to use the bathroom downstairs."

"What if I was in my 90's? I'd have to walk down a flight of stairs?" Now the man was getting impatient with Sam. She had a habit of pushing too far. She decided to let it alone, she really had to go now.

"Lucky for me I'm not 90, eh?" She quickly walked away and looked back to see the man shaking his head, looking like he was unsure of what he was doing before he was rudely interrupted.

After finishing her business in the bathroom, Sam took the opportunity to call her friend, Stacy. She was really going to need a drink after this whole ordeal was over.

"Stacy, hey, how are you doing?"

"Hi, how's it going? You still at the funeral?"

"Yeah, we are at the wake and then we go to the cemetery. They aren't having a mass so we have about another hour here and then we'll head out. And then we are supposed to go back to my mom's, but I don't know, I might just split."

"Really? But, it's your dad." Stacy hesitated to mention that obvious fact to Sam but couldn't believe Sam's unemotional attitude about burying her dad.

"Hey, we all have to die sometime, right?" She laughed but because of Stacy's lack of response, thought she should explain a bit more.

"He wasn't exactly a stellar dad, if you know what I mean."

"No, I guess I don't. My dad was a great dad and I still miss him every day, even though he died almost five years ago. I couldn't even think about him for months after without breaking down."

"Well, you're lucky. My dad was not great. My dad sucked as a dad, from my earliest memories until the end. Maybe he was better for my brother and sister but he sucked for me. I wouldn't have missed him if he left years ago so I certainly don't miss him now that he is dead."

"Wow, well, that is sad, Sam. Yeah, I guess you do need a night out. So, when do you think you'll get here?"

"I don't know, probably around 7, maybe before. We can get a bite to eat and head to Freeky Freddies for a few drinks, some dancing, partying, whad'ya think?"

"OK, sounds like fun. How's your painting coming?"

"Good. OK, I'll see you then. I gotta go before big sister Paula sends out a search party."

"OK, bye."

Sam didn't want to get into a conversation about her painting. Stacy always brought it up. She was sure Stacy meant well but she felt pressure when people kept asking how her painting was going. It was like they were looking for an itinerary on all the galleries she was in, what she has sold, how many new paintings she has and it was too much to think about and then have to answer, none, none, and none to all the questions. It was better to just avoid any discussion at all. She felt like shit about herself as it was, why kick dirt in her face while she was lying on the ground.

Sam took her time walking upstairs and back to the Sawyer party. Looking at the paintings on the walls, she came to the conclusion that they were most likely purchased at Walmart along with the statues, plastic plants, and other tacky furnishings that lined the hallways. She wondered if the bar was open yet. Smiling, she walked back into the room and took her place beside Paula, who was nodding and accepting condolences from Cousin Patty and her husband Don.

"Oh sweetie, I'm so sorry. Your dad was too young, it is awful that he died so young. It must be so awful for you, being the youngest. I always remember you were daddy's little girl. I'm really sorry." Patty hugged Sam so hard and when she looked at Sam's face, tears were running down her face. Sam nearly burst out crying. Not about her dad's death, but about the inaccuracies of most of what Patty just said. She wondered how someone could be so wrong about the way things really are, but then she realized; she didn't know, she just didn't know. No one knew. Everyone here thought her dad, although a drunk - she was pretty sure everyone knew that - was a good guy who just had a drinking problem. He was always the life of the party, a funny guy. No one knew how abusive he really was. How he used to beat Sam with his belt for no good reason and her mother would just stand by helpless. How when he staggered home, falling through the door onto his face, if he thought someone laughed or even smiled he would just start hitting, the fury in him lashing out against Sam and her mom. The bastard! Sam forced the tears down.

"Oh sweetie!" Another big hug from Patty. Sam wished she could tell the truth, tell Patty everything that she didn't know. But she couldn't, she kept it all in for her mom. Her mom knew his family loved him, thought he was a great guy. Sam was pretty sure only she and her mom knew the truth about dad. She knew that now that it was over, that he was finally dead and gone, there was no good reason to bring up the past and reveal the truth about the monster that was her father. Her mother could finally relax and live a better life without him. She couldn't take that away from her mom. She just couldn't.

"I don't think I can do this." Sam whispered to Paula.

"Look, none of us want to do this, but we have to, we have to get through this, for ma. Just get through the cemetery and then you can go get drunk." There it was, the smug, judging face that she just wanted to slap. Sam looked away, resisting the urge to lift her arm and bring her hand down as hard as she could across the pink lipstick smeared on Paula's tight lips.

"I need some air." Sam walked across the room, bumping into Cousin Fran who turned, ready to give a piece of her mind, and then stopped and grabbed Sam, hugging her.

"Oh, I'm so sorry about your dad."

"Thanks." Sam pulled herself away and nearly ran to the door. Outside, she took several deep breaths. Boy, did she need a drink. How was she going to make it through the rest of this day? She wondered if she had time to run to a liquor store and get a six-pack. She just needed to relax. She took a few more deep breaths. She checked her watch, only twenty minutes left for the wake and then they were on to the cemetery. One more trip to the bathroom should take care of that and then they'll be on their way.

Sam went back inside and walked into Paula who was heading outside.

"Hey, where are you going?"

"You aren't the only one who needs some air, Sam."

"Yeah, OK, whatever." Sam walked back into the room and took her place with the family, a short distance from her mom with Jack practically so close she nearly lost sight of her mom right next to him.

Paula walked back in the room and stood next to Sam.

"Can we go now?" Sam was being funny but never knew how Paula would react.

"I hope, what time is it anyway?" Sam looked at her watch.

"3:20, this goes till 3:30, right? So it's over."

"Yeah, I just want to see what mom is doing. I think she wants to drive with me and Ed. Jack probably wants her to go with him and Barb. He's such a pain in my ass."

Whoa, Sam didn't see that coming. She thought Jack and Paula were attached at the hip, cut from the same cloth so to speak. Maybe she was wrong.

"What do you mean?"

"He's so damn controlling, he wants everything to go the way he thinks it should go because he thinks he is always right. A royal pain in the ass."

"Yeah, that's what I always thought, too. I just didn't think that was how you thought."

Jack stood like a sentry next to their mother, shaking hands and hugging all the friends and relatives as they walked out of the funeral home and headed for their cars.

"The dutiful son." Paula whispered to Sam out of the corner of her mouth. Sam smiled as she walked up to her mother and whispered that she was going to her car to get in the funeral line.

"Why don't you come with us, dear. I'm going with Jack and Barb."

Jack glared at her. Obviously he wanted mom all to himself.

"I have to go someplace after so I'm going to take my own car."

"But you're coming back to the house, aren't you?" Her mother had that familiar pained look on her face. Just like the one she had when Sam's father was beating her with his belt. Helpless.

"Uh, yeah, of course, for just a little while but I made these plans weeks ago, before dad died, you know. It's something I can't really get out of." She was speaking quietly to her mom so that Jack couldn't hear. She had her fill of his judging, criticizing looks and wanted only her mother to hear her shabby excuse.

"Well, I hope you do come back for a little while, OK dear?"

"Sure mom."

Sam got in her car and waited with all the others who were heading to the cemetery. She watched her mother walk out with Jack holding her arm as if she couldn't do it without him. Paula followed close behind scowling at the back of Jack's head. Her husband Ed and Jack's wife Barb dutifully followed Paula.

Jack walked over to his car and helped mom into the passenger side. Barb stood there for a second as if she was wondering where she was going to sit and shot Jack a wide-eyed questioning look. Jack said something and opened the back door for her. She stood there defiantly for a few seconds and then got into the back seat. Paula was next and angrily discussed, Sam guessed, why mom was driving to the cemetery with Jack and not with her. Jack wasn't budging, mom was going with him. Paula stood there fuming as Jack got into his car, started it, and pulled in behind the hearse that was carrying the casket.

Sam took a deep breath, happy she wasn't even in the running to bring mom to the cemetery. Besides, she knew she would be mom's last choice since she was the least favorite child. She always chose being with Jack or Paula over her. Even though Sam had lived in her triple-decker apartment for three years now, Sam's mom had been there only once, and that was when she first moved there. She acted like she would catch something if she actually went into her place. Sam imagined her mom showering and throwing her clothes into the laundry the minute she got home in case any cooties climbed onto her while she was at

Sam's. She brought Sam a plate that day, wrapped in paper covered with spring flowers. Apparently something to put cookies on when you had company and served them tea and cookies. It was the most useless gift she had ever gotten. And it made Sam realize, her mom didn't know her at all. She wasn't quite sure where she got the 'dirty' feeling from though since Sam kept her place reasonably clean, sweeping the hardwood floors at least weekly. And it was only four rooms, not like she had to spend hours cleaning such an expansive place. Mom only sat in the living room, too. Sure, she had her easel and paints set up there since this room had the best light. But she had a throw cloth on the floor around it and the sofa and chair were clean enough. Well, they were for Sam anyway, but apparently not for her mom.

The long drive to the cemetery was relaxing for Sam. She enjoyed driving and usually listened to music to drown out the guilt voice. But not today; she heard Jack's voice, then Paula's voice, and finally, her mother's tolerant and patient voice. The one that bothered her the most was, of course, her mother's voice. But, it was more than just that quiet, hesitant, unsure quavering when she spoke to Sam, as if Sam would suddenly backhand her across the face. It was the look also, as if she needed to duck and shield herself. She somehow forgot that Sam was not the violent one in the family, her dad was, the man her mother had protected all these years. She just couldn't put that thought out of her head. Why she would allow him to bruise and beat her child, and herself, to protect what? His good standing in a family of alcoholics and other dysfunctional abusers? Sam turned the radio dial higher and sang along with the radio, ignoring the tears running down her cheeks. She thought it was ironic that she was crying, not for the man who died, but for what had died in her over the years at the hands of the brutal man they were all honoring today. And now she wanted to scream! So scream she did. Screaming and crying came out of her so that she had to pull off the road and out of line of the funeral procession. Of course, those driving by looked at her, shaking their heads knowingly. Poor Sam, she is the youngest and daddy's little girl. She must be taking this so hard. She could hear them all now. Thinking about that just made her angry and the tears stopped.

The last car, a maroon Cadillac, drove by and Sam cleaned up her face, keeping an eye on the Caddy. Most of her mascara had washed off but she looked presentable now and continued on her way, following the Caddy to the cemetery.

They finally pulled into the cemetery and she found a place to park, a long walk off from the actual grave site where everyone had gathered. By the time she got there, the ceremony had already begun. She saw Jack and Paula on either side of mom. Jack gave her his look and shook his head. He took a deep breath and let it out slowly. Paula glared at her, lips thin and tight. Her mother didn't seem to notice that Sam wasn't standing next to them but was across from them, more towards the back of the crowd. Sam felt she was standing in her right place.

As the ceremony came to an end and people took flowers from the floral arrangements placed around the grave, Sam turned, and without saying good-bye, walked away.

Seven Storied Houses

Changing Directions

The day started early at Fielding Farm. Ted and Laura Fielding got up at 4:30 and after making lunches for their 5 kids to take to school and making a hardy breakfast for themselves, the cows needed milking, chickens needed feeding along with the goats, sheep, and horses. And then the real fun began; tending to their 82 acres of organic farmland. Weeding and planting always took the longest. The kids helped out when they returned home from school, after they finished their homework. And of course on weekends everyone was involved in farm work. A hard life for all.

Which would explain why three of the Fieldings, Chris, Jon, and Luke, did not like farm work and had no plans to continue in the family business. But Lilly, at age eight, although not really responsible for too much around the farm, did love to help as much as they would let her. Usually she just got under foot but she knew what needed to be done with the animals and she was a quick learner. She was good at collecting the eggs from under the chickens and spreading corn for them to eat.

The only one who loved farm work and wanted to make this his life was Gary. At twelve years old he had always loved the farm and when he was two he would crawl out among the cows and the horses. They were all gentle with him and the horses, in particular, would nudge him along and out of the way. He had a special bond with them almost from birth.

Christine, the oldest daughter, loved all the animals more than taking care of the fields but she had plans for herself. She was off to college next year and was so excited about majoring in Fashion Design. She made her own clothes and was drawing unique designs every chance she got. She had drawing books full of ideas and couldn't wait to get the training she needed to start working on her own business. She had already set up a website for herself and was getting a lot of interest in her designs on Pinterest and Instagram. Of course, she had very little time to make clothes but during those long winter months when there wasn't anything that had to be taken care of with the fields and her other siblings were helping out with the animals, she would design and make clothes. There wasn't much of anything that gave her more joy than that.

Jon and Luke loved sports and doing the heavy work on the farm, 'to make me strong' as Luke always said. He admired his big brother and even though there was a mere year between him and Gary, he thought of Gary as his little brother and bonded more closely with Jon who was two years older. Chris wondered if Luke really loved sports as much as he said or if it was only because Jon liked playing sports so much. A football star in high school, and only a sophomore, Jon planned on going to college on a sports scholarship. If he didn't make it to football stardom, there was always baseball. He was an all-around star athlete. He didn't play much basketball - mostly because he didn't have time - but he loved the fast pace of the sport. Ted and Laura wished he would get into one of the less physically challenging sports, like baseball or even learn golf, but they knew that football was Jon's first love. It was too soon to tell what Luke would be interested in since he was only thirteen. He would most likely follow in the footsteps of his hero older brother.

Spring started early this year. All the Fieldings were extra busy this time of year because preparations for planting were in order as well as the usual chores with the animals. They had all been doing this for so many years. The farm was passed down from Ted's dad to him and Laura and this was the only place Ted had ever lived. They lived here with his dad, Theo, until he passed away when Chris was 7. Ted's mom had died when he was only 8, the same age Lilly was now. Ted and his brother, Gordon, lived with their dad, helping out at the farm as much as they could. The farm life wasn't for Gordon and he got a basketball scholarship and went to college in upper state New York. And that was where he settled. Married now with two girls, he didn't get much of a chance to visit the farm. And Ted couldn't get away to visit him.

Of course, the farm had been bigger then. They had about 120 acres and several farm hands who worked for his dad. Over the years, with Ted and Gordon growing and Gordon going off to college, and the occasional bad growing season, Theo would sell off a few acres. And then Ted, after marrying and having five kids, also needed to sell off a few more acres. Theo never had animals, except horses that helped plow the land. It was Ted who added the other animals. And Laura also loved having the animals since she, too, had grown up on a farm. Farm life was the only life either of them knew. It was disappointing to them that only Gary and Lily wanted to follow in their footsteps. It was a hard life and both Ted and Laura knew how exhausting it was at the end of the day. Still it saddened them to think the farm might be sold off in their lifetimes. They put all their hope in Gary who talked about nothing but the farm and how he would take care of everything. Although they had hoped their children would love farm life as much as they both did, they also encouraged them to find their true passions.

This was something Ted and Laura had talked about before they married. When they had children, they would not be the kind of parents who insisted their children go into the family business. Theo made it clear that one of his boys would take over the farm; there was no question about it. Gordon saw sports as his out and got what he wanted. And that left Ted to take over the farm. Although he was younger than Gordon by three years, he was always the responsible one. Theo knew he could depend on Ted. Even more so once their mother died. And when Theo got sick with cancer, Ted was there to help with everything Theo needed. Gordon called occasionally, making excuses as to why he "couldn't make it this weekend, sorry I have to cancel. But I'll call again in a few days and maybe I can get up there in a week or two." The saddest part was he never did get up to see his dad until the wake. But, as Ted said, that was something Gordon had to live with. Ted knew he had done everything he could to help his dad.

With the animals fed, the kids were off to school. They walked together down the driveway until they reached the main road where the bus picked them up. Chris and Jon took the 7:10 bus to Mt. Shoal High School. Luke, Gary, and Lilly got the 7:15 bus to Mt. Shoal Elementary. Luke, nearly as tall as Jon, was in his last year at the elementary school. That was fine with him since he felt a little bit embarrassed every time he got on the bus. He thought the other kids must be thinking, 'why is this big kid on our bus?' He was ready for high school and everything it had to offer. Although there was just a year between them, Luke was always much bigger than Gary and since he spent so much time with Jon, who was also big for his age, he appeared to be much older than he was. Of course, Gary thought it was cool to have a big, strong brother walking behind him on the bus. He knew none of the other kids would ever consider bothering him. They knew Luke could kick their asses and most likely their bigger brothers' asses, too.

Little did they all know, though, that Luke was a sweet, gentle soul and had cried when they lost a puppy that came out upside down when Lovey, their Border Collie, gave birth. And yes, Lilly got to name their dog. Lovey was such a love and so snuggly it was the perfect name for her. But of course, she grew up and turned into such a high energy dog it was difficult to imagine her sitting still long enough to get pregnant. But they all wanted another Border Collie so they bred her once and then had her spayed. And now they had Lovey and her son, Oreo, who reminded Lilly of an Oreo cookie since he was black and white. Most Border Collies were that coloring but Oreo's coloring did remind you of the famous cookie with white around his stomach and black at his head and butt.

The kids were all quite popular in school and had full lives both in school and out. Chris wasn't involved in any sports at school but she was a good student and always did her homework, assigned lessons, and even extra credit. She knew what she needed to do to get into college. With so much competition, she wanted to stand out from the others. She was always involved in several clubs, because she knew the recruiters from the various colleges she had applied to looked at these extra-curricular activities favorably. Her favorites were the Art Club, Young Entrepreneurs, and the Senior Book Club. This year she had also joined the Yearbook Committee.

She had applied to two colleges and had already received acceptance letters from both. Her first choice was out of state and as excited as she was to have been accepted she knew this would take her away from everyone she loved.

Chris was in study hall when she felt a kiss on the back of her neck. She was so focused on preparing for her Senior Book Club meeting after school that she jumped. Several of the other students in study hall turned to look at her. Troy jumped over the row of seats in the auditorium and sat in the seat beside her.

"Hello beautiful." That was how he usually greeted her. And it always made her smile.

"Hi Troy. What's up?" She tried to be all business but she couldn't control the butterflies whenever he was around. She was pretty sure this was what love felt like. She also suddenly felt warm and knew her face was telling Troy exactly how she felt about him.

"Oh, not much. But I knew you were in here and I just had to see you. Can you get away tonight? Just for a couple of hours? I want to show you something." Neighbors of the Fieldings, the Melvins grew up just down the road. Troy's brother, Taylor, was the same age as Jon and their youngest, Tomas, was Gary's age. Troy, Taylor, and Tomas all had the initials 'TM'. According to Troy, their grandmother was a hippie and into Transcendental Meditation or TM as it was called in the 60's. A strong woman she had a big influence on her daughter, Tabitha, who married a man whose last name was McDonough. They divorced not long after their last son was born and lived with her parents on the farm, all 225 acres of it. Troy, like Chris, grew up on the family farm. He was going into the family business. More prosperous than the Fieldings, they grew many kinds of vegetables and had fruit trees as well. Their farm was busy almost year round. Chris loved Troy but would never give up her dream of fashion designing for anyone. Not even the boy who held the key to her heart.

"I have a book club meeting right after classes today and then we have chores at home."

"Now, you know, Chicklets, that I know there isn't all that much going on at the farm right now and that what there is to do with the animals, your brothers can take care of it." Chris loved when he called her Chicklets, his pet name for her. He once said there wasn't any gum that tasted as good and as sweet as Chicklets and told Chris she reminded him of sweet, minty Chicklets and so the name stuck. But Chris also knew that they had a lot of farm help at the Melvin farm and the Fieldings did not.

Chris wasn't sure what Troy wanted to show her but she was curious so she would figure something out at home so that she could go to Troy's house.

"OK, I'll come over after my book club and after I check in at home. And then we'll have dinner so it won't be until about 7, OK?"

"No, I can't wait that long. Come for dinner, you know my mom always has plenty."

"Well, if you let her know I'm coming then I will call my mom and tell her I'm going to your house for dinner and I'll find out if they need me at home."

"Perfect, I'll call right now." Troy gave Chris a kiss on her cheek and walked out, taking his cell phone out of his pocket. Chris couldn't concentrate now, wondering what he wanted to talk to her about but also hoping it wasn't what she thought it was. She thought he would ask her to marry him. She was excited and upset at the same time because she loved Troy so much but she was also not letting marriage stop her from going to college. She wanted him to wait. They had talked about it. He was afraid she'd never come back and would meet some fancy college guy who would sweep her off her feet.

After book club Chris took the late bus from school and got off at Troy's house. The smell of fried chicken surrounded the Melvin's farmhouse. Chris took a deep breath as she walked into the house, knocking briefly at the door. She was already one of the family and was always welcome. Since they grew up next door to each other, even though next door was ½ mile away, they were bonded in ways usually only family members are.

"Hello," she called from the front door, wandering towards the kitchen where she often found Troy's mom, Tamel. She went back to her maiden name, Melvin, after she divorced Troy's dad and told the kids, including the Fieldings, that they could call her Tamel. Although her mom had been dead for nearly ten years now, she wouldn't take the name 'Mama Mel' since that was what everyone called her mother. So she made up 'Tamel' which combined Tabitha with Melvin.

"Hello, Tamel, are you in here?" Chris slowly pushed the swinging door into the kitchen. Tamel was standing at the stove, sticking a fork into the boiling potatoes. She turned to face Chris when she walked into the kitchen.

"Oh, hello darlin', come on in. Sit down right there at the table and I'll get you a nice cup of tea. How are you doin' today? Troy was very excited to have you come to dinner tonight. I think he has something special he wants to show you."

"No, no tea, thanks. Yes, he did mention…"

"Where is that boy?" She walked towards the swinging door and pushed it open, standing in the doorway.

"Troy! Chris is here." In the distance she heard a soft 'OK' and then heard heavy footsteps coming down the staircase.

Tamel had gone back to the potatoes and then turned to snap beans at the table.

"Can I help you with those?" Chris reached for the pot that was waiting next to the bowl of green beans. Tamel grabbed the pot away from her and motioned for her to go with Troy.

"I think you should go with Troy, sweetie. I'll see you at dinner. Should be ready in about a half hour or so."

Troy took Chris' hand and escorted her upstairs to his bedroom. He was bubbling with excitement and she couldn't wait to see what he had to show her. They went into his room and he closed the door behind her and then motioned for her to sit on his bed.

"OK, what do you want to show me, Troy?"

He suddenly seemed very nervous. He turned away from her and took something off the top of his dresser. He turned back to Chris but kept what he had in his hand behind his back. He looked so innocent in that moment that it took every bit of Chris' willpower not to jump up and kiss him. Although they had been in Troy's bedroom many times before, he usually kept the door open, house rules. They had some serious necking sessions but so far had not consummated their relationship. They had a magnetic attraction to each other and often found themselves wrapped in each other's arms within seconds after kissing but Chris, always the stronger of the two, would pull away, sit up on the bed, and demand that they get back to studying. As she sat on the bed now she kept looking at the closed door, waiting for it to open or wanting to get up off the bed and open it herself. She didn't trust herself at that moment but even more so, she didn't trust Troy. She wondered how she was able to resist his charms so far and always remembered her goal: fashion design.

"You know, baby, that I love you more than anything in this world. You know that I would do anything for you. And you know that it is my sole purpose to make you happy."

Chris interrupted him at this point, "But you can't make me happy, only I can make myself happy."

Troy had heard this before. "Yes, I know, I know. But you know what I mean. I would do anything for you and how sad I would be if you were sad." She felt like he was rambling now and she was waiting for him to show her whatever it was that he kept hidden behind his back.

Slowly he took from behind his back a piece of paper. He moved towards Chris, got down on his knees and placed the paper into her lap. She was almost afraid to look at the paper, fearing what it might say. He made such a ceremony of it though she decided she needed to look at it. She opened the paper and saw that it was a deed to 80 acres of land, title owned free and clear by Troy McDonough. She was a little confused and wondered why he was giving this paper to her. She looked up at him and the question must have been written all over her face.

"It's for us, baby. My mom said this was left in her parent's will, to be given to me on my 18th birthday. And since I turned 18 not more than a month ago, this is now my… our land. Our land, yours and mine. If you'll have me and be my wife, Chris." Troy then got onto one knee and from under his bed took a small box, opened it, and presented a small but brilliant diamond ring.

"It was Mama Mel's engagement ring and she would want you to have it. But if you don't want this one, I understand, I will get you your own, you can pick out what you want."

Chris was overwhelmed and felt herself warming up, her face felt hot, she thought she was holding her breath and realized she was having a hard time breathing. She was overwhelmed with love for Troy and also with a sadness like she had never felt before. She pulled him to her and they lay wrapped in each other's arms on the bed, holding each other as tight as they could. She wanted this moment to go on forever, to never leave this room, to die this very instant and she would never be happier. But then Troy spoke.

"You haven't said yes, Chris. Please make me the happiest man alive and tell me you'll be my wife."

"Oh, Troy." Chris began to cry.

"Baby, what? Please don't cry. It's your school, right? I know what you want and I want you to have it, too. You can go to school, of course. But I want you to go knowing we will always be together no matter how far away you go or for how long. Please say yes."

Chris continued to cry and held Troy tight. He kissed her face, her tears, and down her neck. She felt him getting turned on and she wanted him to take her right there, in his bedroom, behind his closed door.

"Troy, Chris, supper is ready. Get your brothers, Troy."

They both jumped and started to laugh but continued to hold each other.

"Let's go downstairs. You can wash your face in the bathroom." Troy wiped Chris' face, kissing the tears, her cheeks, her mouth. He pushed her hair behind her ear and stood up from the bed. She took his hand and they walked out of the room together.

In the bathroom Chris did her best to compose herself but felt the urge to cry as loud as she could for as long as she could until she got all of the crying out of her. She got a washcloth out of the towel closet and wetting it, threw it on her face. She didn't want to leave the room and put the toilet seat down to sit. Sucking on a piece of the washcloth she screamed, biting down hard. After a few minutes she heard a knock at the door.

"Babe, are you OK? Everyone's at the table. Come on, let's go downstairs."

She quickly composed herself and opened the door.

"Do I look OK?"

"You always look beautiful to me." Troy took her hand, kissed it, and they walked downstairs to the dining room.

After dinner, Troy and Chris excused themselves so Troy could take her home. They got into his truck and drove to a special place they had, down by the pond that was on his newly inherited land. They had gone here often over the years so they named it their favorite spot. Troy spread a blanket and they lay down together, again wrapped in each other's arms. But this time it was different. It wasn't a desperate clinging but more a need to feel every part of each other against their skin. They both knew this was it. Troy carefully removed her blouse and unhooked her bra. Chris lifted his shirt over his head. They knelt in front of each other, reaching out, touching, caressing. Troy unzipped his jeans and slipped them off. Chris followed his lead. They each removed their underwear and lay down together, kissing, hugging, their bodies aglow with sweat and blood flowing through and into each other coming together and melting as one. Troy wrapped the blanket around them and they lay in each other's arms, neither wanting this particular day, this moment, to ever end.

When he dropped her off at her house they kissed. She started to leave the truck but Troy pulled her back.

"You know, you never gave me an answer. I really need to know. I need to know if you want to be my wife."

Chris leaned in and kissed him on the cheek.

"You know how I feel about you, Troy. I love you more than anything."

"But? I feel like there's a 'but' coming."

"You also know how I feel about fashion design and my plans to go to college in the fall. I have to do it Troy. I will not be happy and would never make you a good wife if I had to give this up. I'm not cut out to be a farmer's wife. I need to have this for myself, separate from what you do. You know how farming is a passion for you, well, that is how fashion is for me. I need this. It means more to me than anything."

"I do understand, Chicklets. I know, I get it. And like I said, you will go to college in the fall as you planned. I want more than anything for you to be happy with our life and I know 'we' won't have a life together if you aren't able to do what you want to do. I'll do whatever I need to do to make sure that happens for you."

Chris loved him so much and wondered what she would do without Troy. She wrapped her arms around his neck and kissed him. He held her tight. The butterflies were so active in her stomach she thought she would be lifted right out of his truck and into her house.

"I love you so much Troy. Thank you for being so understanding and wonderful."

"And….?"

"And, yes, I will marry you, Troy. When the time is right." She jumped out of the truck and blew him a kiss, running into the house.

As the weeks passed, Chris continued with her school projects and farm commitments and Troy busied himself with his new obligations for the land that was now his. He was excited about building a house that would be his and Chris'. He was excited about them starting a life together. But he knew she needed to go to school and pursue her dream of designing fashion. She wanted that more than anything and he wasn't going to stand in her way. He wished it was different but this was the woman he loved and he would do anything as long as she was happy.

He wanted to talk to her about house plans but she was unusually moody and didn't seem to want to discuss anything with him. He left her alone for a few days and when he brought it up again, she was even more irritable.

"So, do you not want to marry me now?" He had to ask.

"Yes, Troy, I still want to marry you. Please let me finish my work, I'm very busy and want to do well so I don't start off my college year behind already." He tried to be patient.

She wasn't sure what was going on; with finals coming up as the end of the school year approached, she thought it was just nerves. But she felt nauseous and thought she needed to change her diet. Maybe she needed more protein. She was tired and made a commitment to get more sleep. She drank more water and thought she just needed to take better care of herself. She finally went to the doctor, alone.

Her parents were exhausted as usual. Chris mashed
the potatoes as if in a trance. The family busied
themselves with setting the table and putting bowls of
green beans, fried chicken, plates and silverware on
the table. Once they were all seated, Chris, sitting next
to her mother who took her usual place at one end of
the table with her dad at the other end, stared into her
plate of food as if searching for an answer in the gravy
that flowed down from the top of the potatoes onto
the plate, surrounding the green beans. She swirled
her fork around the plate, creating a paisley design.
She seemed unaware of the chatter that went on
around her until her mother finally brought her out of
her trance.

"Chris? What's going on?"

Chris jumped when she heard her name and looking
first from her mom and then to the other end of the
table at her dad, with tears now spilling out of the
corners of her eyes and splashing into her gravy swirls,
spreading the brown sauce farther out on the plate
onto her chicken and stopping at the edge of the plate,
made her announcement to everyone at the table.

"I'm pregnant."

Illustration Credits

DJ Geribo –

Cori Caputo –

Barbara Carlson –

Mark Cowper –

Mary Frances Smith –

on the cover

DJ Geribo has been painting for several decades, teaching herself to paint in a variety of mediums. Her favorite subjects are animals, nature, and still lifes featuring fruits and vegetables. She has won several awards for her fine art that she displays at VynnArt Gallery in Meredith, NH and occasionally at other locations around the state.

To see more of DJ's artwork, she invites you to visit her website at www.DJGeribo.com.

DJ also takes commissions for animal portraits which she can create using pastels, oils, or acrylics. To see her animal portrait work, you can visit her website www.animalportraitsbydonna.com.

DJ lives in the Lakes Region of New Hampshire on 27 rural acres with her husband, Jim Fontaine, two Pomeranians, a Miniature Pinscher, and a Goffin's Cockatoo.

Cori Caputo loves to create narrative art that transports the viewer to happy or thoughtful places. Freedom, joy, and humor are common themes in her drawings and watercolors. From mysterious landscapes to enchanted environments, there is something for just about everyone within her portfolio.

She earned her BFA from Alfred University, NY. Since 1984 her work has won awards, been licensed in calendars, puzzles, and featured in galleries from Maine to Virginia. She also has her own line of greeting cards.

To see more of Cori's work, visit her website at www.coricaputo.com.

BARBARA CARLSON

Barbara Carlson is a lifelong artist and Michigan resident. Always experimenting, Barbara works in many mediums, such as watercolor, oils, mixed media, mosaic, pastel, and pen and ink. Her works rarely have a planned outcome as she relies on intuition and allowing the piece to be what it wants to be.

Barbara exhibits in many local and regional art shows, often garnering awards.

Barbara runs an art studio in Grand Haven, Michigan where she curates monthly shows and teaches art classes to children and adults. She is passionate about bringing out the creativity in others and watching them develop. She believes that the creative process is essential to all of us as human beings. The creative process is a journey, and not necessarily important to the outcome of the work.

You can find her work at www.barbaracarlsonart.com and www.armoryartcenter.com and on Facebook.

Mark Cowper
Owner/Artist
Cowper, Ink.
Hilliard, OH

Mark Cowper has been creating pen and ink renditions of houses and buildings for over 20 years. From a young age, he always aspired to be an architect, but desired more creative passions along with developing relationships with clientele. In that timeframe, Mark has produced nearly a hundred renditions that are hanging inside homes all over the United States. Mark's work begins with a detailed, architectural-style, pencil draft that exacts dimensions, as well as perspective. Then all the ink is applied free-hand. The process takes between 40 and 100 hours for each drawing.

To see more of Mark's work, please visit www.CowperInk.com, or contact him at cowperink@gmail.com.

A professional artist specializing in ink and watercolor renderings, Fran finds her passion in portraying buildings and landscapes. So much of who we are is reflected in the places we've lived, worshipped, and celebrated. Her goal is to capture those places in a way that can be saved for generations.

First introduced to drawing while completing her degree in Interior Design at Purdue University, Fran continues to study and explore new mediums and techniques. The combination of her love of travel, design background, and family of builders has given her an interest in structures and cityscapes. She is fascinated with the challenge of trying to capture a sense of place, whether it is a medieval town, an olive grove, or the house down the block.

More of her work can be seen at her website, www.MaryFrancesSmith.com, and at her Etsy shop, www.etsy.com/shop/maryfrancessmith.

About the Author

DJ Geribo, an author and fine artist, lives in the Lakes Region of New Hampshire. After pursuing fine art for many years, DJ decided to focus on her writing and has completed several children's books as well as a non-fiction book. *Seven Storied Houses* is her first collection of short stories.

DJ is currently working on two new books: a novel and another collection of short stories. Since the short stories are vignettes that stem from the characters in the novel, she plans on releasing them together.

DJ's books and art can be purchased from her website at www.DJGeribo.com.

Her books are available on Amazon and can also be purchased directly from the publisher at www.BBDPublishing.com.

To learn about the author's latest books and paintings, we encourage both readers and art collectors to sign up to receive her free quarterly newsletter on her website.

www.ingramcontent.com/pod-product-compliance
Lightning Source LLC
Chambersburg PA
CBHW030430120726

47903CB00003B/888